Harry was never adverse to kissing a likable female, and at that moment, Cordelia was almost pretty. Very gently, he placed his lips against hers.

For such a shy female, Cordelia responded with an unexpected fervor, her arms snaking about his neck, at first hesitantly, and then with all the strength of an awakening passion. Harry, fired by her response, took her in his arms and drew her against him, marveling at how well her small form seemed to conform to the contours of his own, how her lips tasted sweet against his mouth.

At last, his own fine sense of propriety recalled him to his senses. Virginal females had never been in his style, and he felt a hypocrite for the sensations that Miss Hardy seemed to be causing within him.

THE
DOLLAR
DUCHESS

Rebecca Baldwin

FAWCETT COVENTRY • NEW YORK

A Fawcett Coventry Book
Published by Ballantine Books
Copyright © 1982 by Rebecca Baldwin

ISBN 0-449-50305-4

Manufactured in the United States of America

First Ballantine Books Edition: August 1982

FOR HUNT SLONEM,
WITH LOVE.

CHAPTER ONE

The gentleman who presented himself that spring morning at Overslate House was a vision of fashion. His russet curls were pomaded into the very latest mode, his shirt points were high enough to preclude any notion of turning his head from side to side, the finish on his top boots gleamed like mirrors, and the Malacca stick he carried beneath one arm served absolutely no function whatsoever, save to announce to the world that he was quite in the mode of the season. "Good day, Buffet," he said.

Instead of being startled by the appearance of this gentleman, Buffet, who had been butler at Overslate House since the time of the last duke, actually allowed himself to relax his funereal and rigidly correct manner slightly as he said, "Ah, good day, Mr. Beau," and relieved that person of his high-crowned beaver and that useless, if essential, walking stick. "His grace is closeted with Mr. Lacey, his man of business," Buffet added in significant tones as the gentleman paused before the mirror in the hallway to flick an invisible speck of lint from his lapel.

"Is he, then?" Mr. George Southbie, known to the world as Beau, asked, raising one eyebrow, and tearing himself away from his reflection in the mirror. "I shall wait then—no need to show me, Buffet, I know the way—"

But it would appear that Mr. Southbie did not have to dance attendance upon his cousin after all, for at that moment, a door at the end of the hallway opened, and a tall, lean person whose somber garb and grave demeanor announced him to be a man of the City emerged from that chamber, a portfolio case beneath his arm. As the door behind him slammed loudly, the man winced, and with a pained expression strode down the dim hallway toward the door.

"Bad news, Lacey?" Mr. Southbie asked by way of greeting as the man received his hat and gloves from Buffet.

"What else?" Mr. Lacey asked, shaking his head, his agitation making him slightly more voluble than was his usual custom. He shook his head. "Of all my clients, sir, the Overslates have never failed to exasperate me the most, and so I hope you will inform your father, when you happen to see him! Ever since his grace came into his majority—such as it is, sir!—there has been no talking sense into him! I should not be surprised, although I must admit that I would be sorely grieved, to see the ninth Duke of Overslate residing in the Fleet!" He nodded his head several times in indignation. "I only wish that your father had managed to retain the guardianship of the estate—and so I told his grace!"

Beau tried to suppress a smile as the man stormed out the door, but he was unable to prevent himself from exchanging a look with Buffet. "As bad as all of that?" he asked.

The elderly butler unbent enough to nod his head. "The staff has been arrears in wages for most of this quarter, Mr. Beau," he said gravely.

Beau whistled, shaking his head. "I must have come at the right time," he said cryptically. "I shall go and beard the lion in his den. Don't announce me, Buffet, he would only tell you to tell me to go to the devil when he's in one of these moods, you know," he said, his words trailing over his shoulder as he walked down the corridor and rapped sharply on the door.

"Go away!" a voice said from within the study, and Beau entered.

"I suppose," Beau said, closing the door behind him, "that a man has the right to be rude to his own cousin in his own house." He grinned. "Good morning, Harry."

Henry Arthur Gordon Chrisfield, ninth Duke of Overslate, looked up from a massive pile of papers scattered across his desk. His expression had been dark indeed, but seeing his cousin, his somewhat somber face broke into a grin and he rose. "Beau! Thank God! I thought it would be Buffet with yet another stack of bills from the morning post! How do you go on, coz? And how is the ever lovely Susannah?"

"Increasing again, thank you," Beau replied, settling himself into the chair lately vacated by the unhappy Mr. Lacey. "She sends her regards, as do all the children."

"All four?" Harry asked, pushing a hand through his dark hair.

"Five, my boy, five," Beau replied complacently. "Six in September." He smiled at the thought of his large brood. "At least I think it will be six. Let me see, there's young Robert, and Diana, and Jane, and—well, it doesn't signify, really, because that's not what I came to see you about. In the basket again, Harry?"

The duke shrugged ruefully. "Swallowed a spider!" he said frankly, waving at the loose papers on his desk. "Good God, Beau, you have no idea how shocking m'father's debts were—are! And for all of your father's attempts to drill some sense of management into my brain, I'm damned if I can see a way out of it! The expenses of keeping up this place and Overslate Castle are incredible! Imagine this!" He picked up a billet from the pile. "For wax candles, two dozen, seven and six the dozen—where did two dozen wax candles go?"

Beau Southbie, who had received a very comfortable fortune upon his majority and had had the good sense to marry a lady equally comfortable, merely shrugged and, not for the first time, blessed the fortune that had placed him well out of the running for the title and the debts of Overslate. This did, however, recall to him his mission, and he roused himself slightly. "That," he announced, "is what I came to speak to you about, Harry."

The duke's eyebrows rose slightly. "Candles?" he asked.

Mr. Southbie shook his head. *"Not* candles, Harry. Money."

"Money?" Harry laughed, a short staccato sound. "I should certainly be glad of some! What do you suggest? Should I rob the Bristol Mail? Take to being a Captain Sharp?" He sank back into his chair and regarded the papers spread before him glumly. "Why did your father not tell me before I succeeded to my majority just how badly the estate was done up? What is not entailed is encumbered, and what is not encumbered is mortgaged up to the hilt! How did my father manage to run through a fortune in so short a time? It is almost enough to make one glad that he and my mother were lost in that boating accident, before he could ruin us all!"

Anyone else might have been shocked by such callous talk of the late eighth duke, but Beau, raised up with his cousin since they were of an age, knew him well enough to understand Harry's habit of saying exactly what came into his mind, whether he meant it or not.

"Not," Harry continued, "that I blame your father. Uncle Robert did the best he could, but what could he know about the management of estates as vast as Overslate? I've tried my best, Beau, but it seems that every time I think I understand something about estate management or finance, there's yet another development I never dreamed could happen! Cursed bad luck!"

He shook his head. Beau, regarding his cousin from beneath half-closed eyes, took stock of the duke's appearance. They were much of an age, Beau and Harry, approaching thirty, but domesticity and a secure fortune had given Beau a well-fed, well-groomed look, more or less like a happy baby, while, by contrast,

Harry was lean and somewhat grayish. Not that Harry was unhandsome, by anyone's standards. He had the long, narrow Chrisfield features that lent themselves well to the perfect image of what a duke should be. His complexion was olive, his hair was dark brown and fell across his high forehead in waves that Beau's valet sought to imitate with a curling iron. His deep-set eyes were dark gray, beneath thick black brows, and his Roman nose and thin mouth gave him a certain resemblance to the Duke of Wellington in that hero's younger days. He was, to his cousin's fastidious eye, somewhat careless of fashion, but his cravat was neatly if plainly tied, and his military service was betrayed by the propriety of his coat and waistcoat, where only a single fob depended from his watch chain. It was not quite enough to make Beau wince, but he had often wished that his cousin would adopt a more elegant style of dress, more in fitting with his rank as a peer of the realm, albeit a rather down-and-out peer. But there, Beau thought, you couldn't have everything; and he supposed, for what he had in mind, that Harry would simply have to make do with what he had.

Beau took a deep breath and crossed his legs, sinking back into his chair and regarding his cousin steadily. "Marry an heiress," he breathed, and waited for the reaction.

It was all that he could have wished for. Harry's brows shot upward, and a sardonic grin twisted his lips as he leaned back in his own chair and let out a laugh. "By God, Beau! What heiress would have me? Not in the petticoat line at all, as well you know, coz!" He shook his head, and added, with a twinkle in his eye, "Besides, old man, when you married Susannah, you broke my heart, you know."

"Faddle," Beau replied without rancor. "Thing of it is, Susannah's found you an heiress. Very nice young lady. Father was a Hampshire Hardy, grandfather a baronet. Rich as a golden ball, too—no counting her wealth, Harry." Beneath his calm demeanor, he eyed his cousin carefully.

Harry rose from his chair and crossed the floor, pushing a hand through his hair, shaking his head from

11

side to side. "Another one of Susannah's attempts at matchmaking, hey? Good Lord, Beau, when will your good lady realize that I am a singularly bad bargain in the heiress market? Not even the most socially ambitious mama is likely to consider me a good catch for her daughter—not after they've seen the dry rot in the roof at Overslate Castle and the staggering amount of debts my late father managed to run up—and I'm bad ton, dashed bad ton!" Harry shook his head. "I never set foot in Almack's, or attend balloon launchings or rout parties, or parade myself in any of the fashionable fribbles! Don't even take females up in my phaeton in the promenade! No, heiresses are only interested in men who can elevate their social consequence, and I definitely cannot provide that service!"

Since this was true, Beau did not argue the point, only continued to regard his cousin from beneath his eyelids. "But you *are* a duke, Harry. No getting around that. A genuine duke."

"And what of it?" Harry asked, peering out into the overgrown garden. "I might as well be a crofter, for all of that! Being raised a duke leaves one remarkably uneducated for anything! I am even a failure at estate management—or at least, it will take me another ten years to set right what m'father mismanaged, my bailiff tells me!"

"Thing of it is," Beau said slowly, "the lady in question ain't perfectly tonnish herself. That's not to say she ain't respectable, because she is, and a lady to her fingertips, but there is one small difficulty."

"And, what might that be?" Harry asked, turning slightly from the window, his curiosity snagged at last.

Mr. Southbie cleared his throat. "Well, she's American."

"*What?*" Harry demanded, regarding his cousin as if he were escaped from Bedlam.

Beau coughed discreetly into his fist. "Well, her mother was American, and she was raised up in America, you see, but her father was the son of this Hampshire baronet, a *younger* son, Harry, who went to America to make his fortunes, and did amazingly well at it—"

12

"An American?" Harry demanded again, his eyebrows almost reaching his hairline. "Is this your idea of a very bad joke, old man?"

"Not at all," Beau said, calmly. "Thing of it is, Susannah met her at some tea or another, and took a fancy to her."

"Good God," the duke said with loathing. "Another one of Susannah's strays. Mark my words, this female will toad-eat you both within an inch of your lives—"

"Not like that at all," Beau said stubbornly. "A quiet sort of female, very genteel gel. Wouldn't have known that she could buy and sell us all if Susannah hadn't taken tea with her and her father at Claridge's—the best suites there. Mr. Hardy's a very warm man, Harry—a regular New World nabob! New World nabob—rather like that phrase, must remember it! Yes!"

"Beau!" the duke said dangerously, and Mr. Southbie collected himself from a poetic reverie. "This is preposterous! D'you realize what you're suggesting? Overslate!"

"This is the first time I ever knew you to be overconcerned with the consequence of your title, Harry! Doing it too brown!" Beau remarked, selecting a paperweight from the desk and turning it over in his hands. "Anyway, as I was about to say, Mr. Hardy is anxious—most anxious—to see his daughter fired off as a peeress. And willing to stand the blunt quite handsomely for the privilege, I might add. The dry rot in the roof at Overslate would be *that* to him!" Beau snapped his fingers. "He's a very warm man, Harry—*very* warm!"

"Victor and Dorothea—" Harry began, but Beau shook his head.

"Your brother and sister provide an excellent argument for you to marry well and soon! Got to think of their futures, too, you know! Victor'll be wanting a pair of colors when he comes down from Harrow, and Dorothea's about ready to be launched into society. Can't expect to fire her off in a proper match without a *dot,* can you?"

Harry stopped, biting his lip. His younger brother and sister, a lively pair of sixteen-year-old twins who had come into his guardianship when he had attained

13

his majority, were providing an extreme drain on his resources. Although he felt a deep bond of brotherly affection toward them, he was also quite aware that as the head of the house, it fell upon his shoulders to be sure that they were provided for, and it was not in his power to deny them any reasonable request over and above their school fees and their quarterly allowances. In his view, it was unfair to tax them for the peccadilloes of their father. "Something will arise! They have their portion of Mother's estate—"

"Which is not half enough!" Beau pointed out. "Three hundred pounds a year would barely pay for Dorothea's court dress, let alone Victor's majority!"

For this Harry had no reply, but as he turned from the window to look at his cousin, Beau saw anguish written on his face. "Not a marrying man!" he said, pulling his trump card. "Never was in that line!" He shook his head. "Besides, an American! It isn't done!"

"Cut rope, old boy!" Beau advised. "Never knew you to care for that! Besides, it is time you was becoming a benedick with a nursery of your own to fill, before you put Victor's nose out of joint! There! If you want to talk of duty, it is your duty to marry! You ain't in love, are you?"

Harry shook his head. "Good God, no! Well, there was a gel in Portugal, but that don't signify! Not at all in the petticoat line!" he repeated, running a finger beneath his stock unhappily. "An American!" It was not that he knew anything about America or Americans, save that England had been involved in a recent and rather unfortunate conflict with the former colony. It was not that he was averse to money that could bolster the sagging fortunes of the house of Chrisfield. It was, he finally realized, that having attained the age of nine and twenty in perfect harmony with his own single state, the idea of marriage, even a marriage of convenience with the daughter of a golden ball, made him feel as if a noose were being tightened about his neck. "Dollars!" he said in a quavering voice.

"Pounds or dollars, what's the difference?" Beau asked casually. "The point is, the lady's father has a great fancy to see his daughter a duchess, and he's got the ready to pay for the peerage! Not that I see much fun in being a peeress m'self—m'mother-in-law's continually complaining about all the trappings for the Coronation and the Investitures. But since no English gel will have you, Harry, why not an American? Better than a Frenchie or a Russian, I'd say—and the Hardys have good blood!"

"Good blood," Harry repeated, pushing his hand through his hair. "Good blood!"

"Miss Hardy's blood is excellent. Understand her mother's people were one of the best families in Baltimore, or wherever! You'll take to her, Harry—she's a very genteel gel, well brought up! Never give you cause to blush." Beau added thoughtfully, "Her manners are far better than yours, actually."

"But my manners don't have to be good!" Harry retorted with a grin. "I am Duke of Overslate!"

"And you'll be Duke of Fleet Street soon enough if something's not done, my boy! What did those showy grays cost you, first and last?"

"Leave my horses out of this!" Harry retorted, but he thrust his hands into his pockets and looked very much like a sulky schoolboy as he regarded the pile of bills, which had not miraculously disappeared from his desk in his absence.

"Well, if you have a better solution, I'd like to hear it!" Beau said roundly. "Here, Susannah has found you a top-of-the-trees heiress, even if she is American, well, half American, and you're turning up your nose at the proposition! Better men than you have made marriages of convenience, Harry, and still hold up their heads in society!" For emphasis, Beau reached across the desk and took up a handful of bills, waving them in the air. "If you won't listen to reason, perhaps you ought to listen to necessity! Disgrace the entire family if you was to be thrown into the Fleet!"

Harry blanched, regarding Beau closely. "Well, I don't suppose it would hurt to at least meet her," he said at last, and his tone was grudging. "But I'm not in the petticoat line! I don't know how to pay fancy addresses to females—or any of that!"

Beau smiled. "Thought you'd see it my way," he

murmured complacently. "Tonight for dinner at eight? *En famille,* of course. Just you and I, and Susannah, and Mr. and Miss Hardy. And, of course, Miss Featherstone to make up the table."

"Miss Featherstone! Beau, no!" Harry exclaimed, shuddering at the thought of the Southbies' governess, a most formidable *grande dame.*

"At eight, then," Beau said with a smile as he rose from the table and allowed the sheaf of bills to cascade down upon the mahogany surface of the desk.

"Outflanked!" Harry murmured as he watched the papers drifting like snow and heard Beau whistling cheerfully as he made his exit.

CHAPTER TWO

"It is civil, most civil indeed, of Mrs. Southbie to take you up under her wing," Mr. Augustus Hardy informed his daughter as their huge coach drew up before the portals of Portland Square that evening.

"Yes, Papa," Miss Cordelia Hardy said obediently, twisting the strings of her reticule between her fingers and looking down at the fur lap robe that covered her evening cloak.

"I only wish," Mr. Hardy continued, somewhat wistful, as he was wont to be upon those occasions when his daughter went out to some engagement or another, "that your dear, poor mama were still alive to see how prettily you've turned out."

"Oh, Papa, I wish you would not say that! I am not now, nor have I ever been, pretty, and well you should know!" Cordelia protested softly.

But Mr. Hardy seemed not to hear her. "Your mama was a lady to her fingertips, God rest her soul, and Cordy, my dear, while I've tried to do my best for you these past twenty-seven years, there are some things that only a mother can accomplish." He patted his daughter's hand, and Cordelia managed to summon a tiny smile she was far from feeling.

"I know, Papa," she said. "You have tried to do your best for me—and I am grateful."

Mr. Hardy shook his head. "Everything that money could buy, I've given you, my dear, and you know that there's no other soul on this earth who means as much to me as you."

"Yes, Papa," Miss Hardy said, knowing what was coming next and dreading it. "It would make me as pleased as a toby jug to see you properly established in London society, with a good, sound husband of rank and title to lend you his name. With your fortune, and your birth, Cordy, there's no telling how high you might look for a husband, and it's very kind of Mrs. Southbie to invite her cousin Overslate to dinner tonight."

Miss Hardy flushed up to the roots of her hair, turning her face slightly away from her papa so that he would not catch a sight of her expression in the passing lights of the new gas fixtures. "It is very kind of Susannah to ask us to dinner," she said diplomatically, but suddenly her thoughts could no longer be contained, and she turned, laying a hand upon her father's large paw. "I know that Susannah, Mrs. Southbie, has been more than kind to me, and I do consider her to be my *friend,* Papa, perhaps the only true friend I have made in London. But you know that I cannot help but feel discomfited by London society. These people live in a world very different from what I am used to—their values, their manners, their very ideals are totally alien to what I am accustomed to. Papa, you cannot make a silk purse from a sow's ear, and you cannot force these people to accept me into their ranks!"

Such a display of force was not what was generally expected from quiet Cordelia Hardy, but her papa knew that she could take notions into her head and become quite stubborn about them.

He was not at all discomfited by her speech, and merely patted her hand, adjuring her not to be a goose. "After all, you have gone everywhere and met everyone who matters since we came to London, and if only you would be a bit more forthcoming, Cordelia, I am sure that you would find yourself many more friends."

Mr. Hardy, bred up among these people, was oblivious to the agony that had accompanied almost every waking moment Cordelia had spent since her arrival in England. It seemed to her that fate had conspired to punish her for her very real enjoyment of their travels on the Continent. There the Hardys had been accorded every respect from the most exalted persons they chanced to encounter, and she had been able to move about, if not with an easy grace, at least with a degree of self-assurance that she had been far from feeling since they had set foot on her father's native soil. Augustus Hardy, perhaps, might be oblivious to the sneers that lay beneath the smiles, and the slights that had been subtly cast their way by persons of so-called quality, but Cordelia, ever aware of such things, knew that she had been castigated as an American nobody, attempting to toad-eat her way into the exclusive circles to which her father sought reentry. She was aware that she was considered a parvenu, a vulgar mushroom who did not, and never would, fit into those tightly closed ranks, and not even Augustus Hardy's claim to aristocratic connections could cover up the fact that his vast fortunes had been acquired in trade. That commerce should be considered beyond the pale by these people she found incomprehensible, for in America, it was expected that a person should rise upon his own merits in the world, and to have attained such a distinction was considered admirable. She had noted the raised brows, the polite smiles hidden behind the fans, and the deep wounding she had felt made her become even more retiring than usual. That her father had taken the notion into his head that she should marry into this society seemed quite mad to her, but not for the world would she hurt his feelings by pointing out the signal agonies that had been her lot. She knew how much this visit meant to him, and she would have considered herself heartless and ungrateful if she had pointed out to him that she was less than the rage of the season. Where his daughter was concerned, Augustus Hardy, so shrewd in every other respect, was

19

amazingly blind, and she was resolved to endure this visit stoically, counting the days until they set sail for America again to all that was dear and familiar.

But even such mild protest as Miss Hardy was moved to utter sailed free of her father's sensibility. His florid face had taken on the look of a petulant child, and his large hand slid from his daughter's to retain its grasp on his heavy walking stick. "You are as good as, if not better than, any of them, Cordy, and you hold to that, and keep your head high! My people are the Hardys of Hampshire, baronets as far back as anyone can see, and your mama's people were good solid English stock, one of the best families of Baltimore! What's more, you're as rich as any female in this kingdom, and your papa's a warm man, as full of the brass as will hold! Now, Cordy, with this Duke of Overslate, I want to see you in your best form!" It was upon the tip of his tongue to inform his daughter then and there that hopes were cherished for a match between Cordelia and a man she had never before set eyes upon, but Mr. Hardy wisely restrained himself, and he merely patted her hand, putting off for tomorrow what should have been done yesterday. For all of her retiring manners, Cordelia could be led, as he was fond of saying, but not driven, and she had some definite ideas in her own head about such things. Augustus Hardy, who had some awareness of his daughter's notions or propriety, was hopeful that the thing would take a natural course.

"Look up, girl, we're here!" he contented himself with saying as the footman opened the carriage door to allow Miss Hardy to descend from the carriage.

A few minutes after the Hardys had been admitted to Portland Square, the Duke of Overslate presented himself to these same portals with the air of a man going to the gallows. His valet, following the rumors that were circulating belowstairs, had done his best to turn out his master in a properly suitorly fashion. Certainly not even such a notable dandy as Beau Southbie could find fault with his silk stockings, black breeches, and corbeau-colored coat of bath superfine, and his dove-gray waistcoat was admirable in the extreme. If Hoby had taken the liberty of tying his master's cravat in the style known as the Trône d'Amour, it was to be seen as a gesture of hope, for the story of Miss Hardy's riches had raised that emotion within the breasts of those who wished him well. If the duke was not complete to a shade, he was at least properly attired—or had been so when he had left Hoby's capable hands.

Treedle, the Southbies' ancient butler, solemnly greeted the duke, leading him up the long staircase to the drawing room, his impassive countenance in no way betraying his sense of outrage at this unprecedented state of affairs. But even as the butler's hand was upon the knob, the unmistakably nasal twang of an American accent assailed Harry's ears, and, indeed, fairly rattled the door panels. Treedle winced visibly and closed his eyes.

"—said to him, 'Well, sirrah! I shall buy up all eighty hogsheads, but at seventeen shillings the barrel less than what you've been gouging out of Crombell and French, or any other Yankee merchant fool enough to deal with you! Rum! Rum indeed,' I said, 'that is swill and not fit for sailors on shore leave—'"

Harry squared his shoulders manfully. No green officer facing his first battle could have marshaled more bravery in the face of the enemy than Harry, as Treedle, flinging open the doors, announced the Duke of Overslate in funereal accents, and left Harry to the stares of interested persons arranged about the Southbies' drawing room.

Mrs. Southbie, a deceptively frail blonde with disconcertingly penetrating eyes and early signs of her sixth interesting condition, immediately rose from her chair, trailing a great deal of Brussels lace in her demi-train. Mr. Southbie, correct to a fault in his somber evening attire, nodded his approval of his cousin's haberdashery, and Miss Featherstone, a female of indeterminate years employed as the Southbies' governess through two generations, gave an audible sniff of disapproval. But Harry's attention was immediately drawn to the gentleman in the center of the room, whose presence seemed to dominate the company from his position on the hearthrug, leaning comfortably against the mantel. One hand held a glass of sherry, the other was engaged in keeping his coattails from singeing in the fire. This person's eye fell upon the duke, and for the first time in his life, Harry had the uneasy feeling that he was being weighed up, evaluated, and measured as if he were a piece of livestock at a county fair, being judged for blood, breeding, and aspect.

A flush crept in Harry's cheeks, and he automatically raised his quizzing glass to his eye, only to find that this gesture in no way incapacitated the other man's cursory stare. This, Harry decided, must be Mr. Augustus Hardy, the New World nabob.

Although Harry was only of medium height, he found himself fairly towering over Mr. Hardy, who was of a short and stocky build, rather like a bull terrier. Harry was forcibly put further in mind of that beast by Mr. Hardy's countenance, which was florid and rather jowly, rendered even more distinctive by a pair of small, shrewd eyes set beneath enormous bushy brows. What hair remained upon his head was snow white, and swept back from a gleaming pate. His evening attire, while correct, was startling by the addition of a bottle-green waistcoat, heavily embroidered with flowers, stretched across an enormous belly and strained almost to the breaking point, seemingly held in place by a heavy gold watchchain from which a number of dems, seals, and fobs depended. In the folds of his snowy cravat, over which his several jowls depended, a diamond the size of an idol's eye glittered and winked.

Susannah, a hopeful gleam in her eye, was performing the introductions, and Harry found his hand grasped in a crushing paw. "An honor indeed," Mr. Hardy was booming, almost cracking the bones of Harry's hand as he pumped it up and down, his native Britannic accents almost completely submerged beneath the years of his sojourning in America, "although you are not quite what I expected. Knew your late mother. You favor her," Mr. Hardy continued, as if this were an achievement of Harry's.

The duke raised an eyebrow as he allowed his glass to depend upon its ribband, trying to conceal his astonishment at this rather odd person. It was perhaps fortunate that Harry was momentarily stunned by the sheer presence of this remarkable person, for Mr. Hardy seemed oblivious to Harry's astonishment. Or perhaps he did not care, for he knew very well that he held all the cards, and that Harry was the one on trial.

"And this, Overslate," Susannah said quickly, taking her cousin's arm and leading him across the carpet, "is my friend Miss Hardy. Cordelia, my dear, may I present you to the Duke of Overslate?"

For the first time, Harry was made aware of a second presence upon the settle where Miss Featherstone held court, and he caught a glimpse of a damsel shrinking slightly behind that lady's bulk.

With a little rustle of her skirts, the daughter of Augustus Hardy rose to her feet and dropped a small curtsy, flushing deeply, her eyes seemingly held captive by the shine upon his pumps.

The duke bowed very properly over Miss Hardy's hand, and she stammered in a small, colorless voice that she was pleased to make his acquaintance before settling back into her hiding place behind Miss Featherstone.

If Mr. Hardy seemed to overflow the room's boundaries, Miss Hardy might have been invisible.

All afternoon, Harry's imagination had steeled him for the worst; visions of a large, rawboned creature with simpering airs and a braying voice rendered hideous his hours; but nothing in his imagination had prepared him for the mouselike creature who cowered before him, obviously as discomfited by this situation as was he.

Indeed, "mouse" was an appellation that seemed to suit Miss Hardy to a stroke. It was easy to see that she had inherited her father's small stature, for she barely reached his chin. Her hair, dressed in two neat bands about her heart-shaped face, was of an indeterminate shade of brown, and a diamond-and-pearl clip, set among the curls piled high on her head, did very little to enhance its color. Her features, while by no means repellent, were, in fact, somewhat reminiscent of a mouse. A rather charming mouse, of course, the duke thought judiciously, but a mouse nonetheless. She was possessed of a pair of large brown eyes, a small mouth,

23

and a retroussé nose that he could easily imagine quivering. No one, even in the wildest rapture, could say that she was a beauty, but, to Harry's relief, she was far from being the gorgon of his imagination. Nor was her height increased by her dinner gown, in the latest Parisian mode, with mutton sleeves and a deeply banded hem trimmed in several flounces and ribbands, all in a rather ill-chosen shade of lilac. From the lobes of her ears there pended a pair of baroque pearls, and about her throat she had looped several rows of pearls together with a diamond tremblant.

Not one of Harry's ancestresses could have been said to be a beauty, but all of them had been possessed of the dignity and composure that were to be expected of the lady who bore the title Duchess of Overslate. Harry's imagination, having been divested of the image of the Medusa, was suddenly stricken down once again by the thought of this creature innocuously presiding over the long table at Overslate Castle, and he hastily suppressed a rather cowardly urge to recall a previous engagement and seek out the company of his cronies at his club.

It was only when he allowed his eyes to meet those of Miss Hardy and saw his own acute discomfort reflected in those dark depths that his innate sense of chivalry prevailed, and he permitted her one of those rare smiles of his, his own eyes seeming to say, *What a particularly odious situation we find ourselves in, you and I*, as if this were a jest they shared together.

Miss Hardy relaxed slightly and allowed herself to smile a little at the duke, as to reply, *Indeed, sir, most peculiar!*

And in that moment, Harry found Cordelia almost intriguing.

"Mr. and Miss Hardy have just returned from a long Continental journey," Susannah said, gracefully indicating to Harry that he was to be seated in the chair beside Miss Hardy, and handing him a glass of sherry. If she entertained great hopes from this meeting, she was wise enough to suppress them behind a polite mask, but her clever eyes missed nothing, and so far she was satisfied with her handiwork.

"That's all right and tight!" Mr. Hardy boomed genially, settling himself into a chair beside the hearth, throwing one leg across the other with a vast ease. "I've been giving Cordelia the Grand Tour—Rome, Naples, Venice, Florence, Leghorn, Hesse, Baden-Baden, Copenhagen, Madrid, Paris—quite a change from the days when my brother and I were bear-led by our old tutor, if I do say! Everything first-rate all the way! Trust you know m'brother, duke? Sir Edward Hardy of Hampshire?"

Before Harry could murmur that he had not had this pleasure, Mr. Hardy had plunged in again. "Yes, all first-class, and nothing but the best of everything for my Cordelia! Whatever she had a fancy for, I bought her! Outfitted her in latest Parisian modes! Nothing's too good for m'daughter!"

"Papa," Miss Hardy said quietly, but Papa only shook his giant head.

There seemed to be no reply that the duke could make to the last remark of the merchant prince, so he turned toward the daughter. "And did you enjoy your trip, Miss Hardy?" he asked, hoping to elicit some response.

The curls on either side of her face nodded and bobbed as she inclined her head. "It was very interesting," she whispered.

"And very profitable, I might add!" Mr. Hardy boomed, patting his straining waistcoat as if he carried the profits in his pockets. "Now that they've finally put Boney away where he'll do no more harm, the time's all right and tight for trade again! Imports and exports, that's the ticket! Spanish wines, English wool, Italian silks..." He nodded, and the duke found his dislike of Mr. Hardy growing into a positive loathing.

But Mr. Hardy, with his usual eye for the main chance, had managed to combine his daughter's finishing tour of Europe with his own business ventures, and between regaling the company with tales of war-ravaged countries making their way into the modern era of industrialization, and several accounts of his own shrewd enterprises, which, he let it be known, had added considerably to his already overwhelming for-

25

tunes, quite left the duke at a loss for a suitable response. Indeed, he was hard pressed to decide whether Augustus Hardy was the most appalling bore he had ever encountered in his life, or the biggest braggart. But Harry was under no illusions as to why Mr. Hardy had chosen to impress the company with his derring-do as a merchant prince; it was clear that he was instantly apprising the duke of his vast personal wealth.

From the corner of his eye, Harry noted that Miss Hardy followed this oration with downcast eyes, picking at her chicken-skin fan, a faint flush of color rising in her cheeks. What her thoughts upon all of this might be it was impossible for the duke to determine, but as Mr. Hardy's speeches had allowed no one else to enter into the conversation, there was no opportunity to assay her opinions—if, indeed, she had any opinions at all.

The duke was pressed to conceal an audible sigh of relief when Treedle, at his most morbid, announced that dinner was served, and the company adjourned to the dining room. His hostess ruthlessly suppressed any attempt he might have made to have an underword with her by announcing to the company in general that they would be dining *en famille* tonight, quite informally, since they were all friends, after all.

This hospitable homily was rejoined by Mr. Hardy in his most jovial accents as he allowed Mrs. Southbie to seat him beside her. "Quite all right, dear ma'am! No need to make apology! Plain cooking and plenty of it, that's the way I like to see things done, and I've never known you to set a poor table! M'daughter's been trained up in the domestic sciences, and she can keep household as shrewd as she can hold!"

The duke gritted his teeth, wondering if the man had been so long in America as to forget that no duchess would ever be expected to as much as see the inside of the kitchens, let alone dress a joint.

He was relieved to find that Susannah, in her infinite wisdom, had placed him as far from Mr. Hardy as possible, his view of that gentleman being blocked by the vast silver epergne that graced the center of the table. To Hardy's right was Miss Featherstone, who could be counted upon to sniff with disapproval whenever Beau made some comment with which she disagreed. Miss Featherstone might be a mere governess in the Southbie household, but she had been Mrs. Southbie's governess before assuming control of her children, and as General Featherstone's daughter, was quite capable of holding her own in any company, even that of a visiting American nabob. To Harry's left, Susannah had placed herself as a buffer, and upon his right sat Miss Hardy, flanked between her would-be suitor and her host, ready at her rescue should her conversation flag.

Susannah's modesty about her simple supper *en famille* was instantly betrayed by the arrival of the first course, a terrapin soup ladled out by the first footman into Derbyshire bowls. Harry, seeking to make conversation with Miss Hardy, politely inquired how she found London, and was rewarded, from across the board, by a reply from Mr. Hardy.

"We've been here about a fortnight, your grace, and we've been putting up at Claridge's," Hardy boomed, dabbing at his lips with a napkin. "I've procured the best suites in the house from them—nothing but the best for my daughter, you know! It's been thirty years and more since I've set foot in Merrie Old England, so to speak, and it's been enough to renew old acquaintances and see old friends once again! I've been anxious that Cordelia have a taste of London life, you know! She's been to Almack's, and presented at court—up to every rig and row in town!"

Miss Hardy looked down at her soup, her spoon poised in the air, her expression unreadable. She did not look much like a female who was up to every rig and row in town, the duke thought.

"My Cordelia, after all, could look as high as she pleases to make a match, y'know," Mr. Hardy continued, giving Harry the sudden, uneasy feeling that in his greed to advance his daughter, given half a chance and the removal of the Acts of Settlement, Mr. Hardy would have married Cordelia off to a royal duke, if any of those doddering, debt-ridden brothers could have been enticed to offer their hands in marriage.

"I was hoping, y'know, that m'brother, Sir Edward

27

Hardy, would have obliged me by marrying a woman who moved about in society, but he's turned into an old squire, all hounds and horses, living down in Hampshire single-stated," Augustus Hardy continued, shaking his head ruefully. "You would think, after all these years, and all the money that I've pumped into the old home, he could have at least married to oblige me! A lady who could sponsor m'daughter in society!"

In spite of his best manners, the duke found his lips twitching slightly, and he looked toward his cousin, hoping to catch a like spirit in Beau. But that gentleman was in conversation with Miss Hardy, and loftily ignored him. "M-most unfortunate, sir!" the duke managed to say in tones of such sympathy that Susannah was forced to give him a very sharp look across the board.

Mr. Hardy nodded emphatically, bestowing a broad smile upon his hostess. "Exactly so, duke! But it is most fortunate that my Cordelia has a friend like Mrs. Southbie to take her up beneath her wing, for I don't scruple to say that Mrs. Southbie is up to every rig and row in town, and dashed tonnish!"

Susannah's cheeks flushed with pleasure, and she smiled genially upon Mr. Hardy. "I feel quite fortunate to have made a friend of Cordelia, Mr. Hardy," she replied. "Your daughter is a lady of whom you have every right to be proud."

Mr. Hardy beamed with pride, and did not disagree. Harry was a little surprised to see his cousin's wife, normally, in his opinion, a very sensible, well-bred sort of female, actually seeming to *enjoy* the company of this man.

Susannah extended her smile to include Miss Hardy, and the duke, following her look toward his dinner partner, could not help but note that lady seemed to be undergoing several different varieties of exquisite agony, brought on by her father's blunt speeches. But sensing his look, when she chanced to glance in his direction, he thought that he recognized a sort of challenge in her eye, as if she were daring him to think her papa a vulgarian. It was only the flicker of a look, before her attention was distracted by a question placed

28

to her from Susannah, but it was sufficient to command the duke's respect for Cordelia Hardy. A lesser daughter would doubtless have been thrown into an overflowing fit of the vapors at such plain speech from a parent to a potential suitor. So the little mouse had loyalty and pride, Harry thought, and liked her the better for it. He had seen too many young ladies blush for the manner of their less fortunate parents whose fortunes had paid for their entrance into society.

Cordelia's only reply was a quick, fleeting smile in the direction of Susannah's face before dropping her eyes quickly toward her soup plate.

The duke noted that a small line had appeared between her brows, and again he wondered what went on behind that silent little facade, what thoughts Miss Hardy cherished.

Unfortunately, the opportunity to explore this theme with the lady was denied to him by the removal of the soup course, to be replaced with an excellent Dover sole, and the duke felt constrained, by politeness, to address his conversation toward his cousin's wife. But Mr. Hardy continued to address his remarks across the table to the general company. "Of course, Cordy's never been anything but *out*," he said, dabbing at his lips with his napkin. "Been presented everywhere—Washington, New York, Rome, Paris—but London's the crowning jewel, no, Cordy?"

"Yes, Papa," Miss Hardy agreed tonelessly, as if this series of presentations had been a series of continuing tortures, with London as the *coup de grace*. It would appear that her debut into London society was not her high point, but that of her parent.

"It was Mrs. Southbie who procured her Almack's vouchers! The old tabbies who run that place are dashed high in the instep about just who they'll allow to cross their portals, but Mrs. Southbie pulled it off! I want the proper thing for my Cordelia—nothing second rate or nip-cheese, no matter what the dibs!"

"Papa," Miss Hardy said faintly, but it was sufficient to make that man retire from the conversational lists and confine his conversation, most properly, to Miss Featherstone.

29

Susannah was swift to detect her friend's discomfort, for, making a delicate cut into her filet, she allowed her shrewd blue eyes to rest a second on her friend's face. "Cordelia carries herself very well, you know," she remarked. "She is an excellent dancer."

Miss Hardy cast a rather startled look at her friend, and Susannah smiled encouragingly. "Lady Jersey and Countess Lieven were most particular in their attentions toward her, you know," she remarked, and Harry reflected, not for the first time, what an admirable general had been lost to the world when Susannah had been born of the female sex. It was easy enough to picture Susannah genteely bullying those two august dames into dispatching the all-important vouchers to an insignificant American nobody with only a great deal of money to recommend her.

"I—I do not care very much for society, you know!" Miss Hardy suddenly blurted out, and then dropped her eyes again toward her plate, her face suffused with a scarlet hue.

"This is true, but you are such fine company, Cordelia, that society comes to you! The children adore you, you know—you are so very good with them!" And without missing a beat, Susannah complacently launched into one of the latest and most shocking *on-dits* of the season, smoothly covering her friend's gaffe beneath the flow of her own conversation.

It was only when the sole was removed for a succulent *veal d'ange* served with oyster sauce and a remove of asparagus in truffles that Harry was able to turn his attention toward Miss Hardy again and attempt to acquaint himself with the lady Susannah had chosen to be his future bride. He was beginning to feel that his time might have been better spent in attempting to extract teeth from a hen, for Miss Hardy was addressing her own attention to pushing a morsel of veal about her plate.

"If you do not care for society, Miss Hardy," he said in what he sincerely hoped was a lightly bantering tone, "pray tell me what you do care for!" But the words, coming off his tongue, sounded stiff and stilted in his own ears, and he was forced to recognize his own lack of practice in the art of courtship. This business of paying suit to heiresses was harder than he had expected, he thought unhappily.

Cordelia took a deep breath, regarding him a little warily. It was always thus, she thought miserably, struggling to make light banter with some unfortunate gentleman, when she felt so painfully tongue-tied. Not for the first time, she cursed her own shyness. It was upon the tip of her tongue to reply, *America!* But somehow she felt that this might offend him, so she dropped her eyes and considered for a moment before blurting out, "Oh, the theater—and the arts—and the sights of London, of course!" Having managed this, she felt a little better and was encouraged to peer up at the duke again.

"Have you seen much of our theater?" he tried, a little awkwardly.

Miss Hardy shook her head. "Not so very much," she replied. "Papa is very busy with his affairs, and most of what I have seen of London has been a series of drawing rooms and ballrooms. I did see Mr. Kean's Lear, and it was most edifying," she added. "I mean to arm myself with a guidebook, however, and set off to see the sights."

Harry found the image of a young lady of quality— even an American—tramping about the streets of the city, with the assistance of nothing more than a guidebook, profoundly shocking. Although the duke hoped that he was well-bred enough not to betray this to the lady, his expression nonetheless gave him away.

"American females, your grace," Miss Hardy said carefully, "are used to a great deal more freedom than their English sisters. And I am no longer a schoolgirl. Besides, I shall have my maid with me, and Betty and I shall procure a hackney coach, and I am certain that we shall manage," she said gravely.

"A—a hackney?" the duke's eyebrows rose. In all of his several summers, he had never heard of a lady going about the city with no escort save her maid, in a hackney coach.

"A hackney," Miss Hardy repeated calmly, watching the duke's reactions to her plans for her own entertainment with a certain perverse amusement, all of her shyness nearly forgotten. "We contrived quite well in other cities, after all. And if I asked to use the coach, Papa would doubtless insist that I take Shadwell along with me," she added, more to herself than to the duke.

"Shadwell?" he asked, all at sea.

Miss Hardy permitted herself a little smile, rather enjoying seeing the duke jolted out of his complacency. "Gunther Shadwell is my father's secretary. He has the greatest horror of things that are not American, you see, and this entire journey has taxed his sensibilities terribly, because everything is so—foreign to him!"

Given a little encouragement, Cordelia could forget her self-consciousness, and she was a little animated as she described her plans to Harry. It was becoming to her, and, drawn into her confidences, Harry felt a definite sense of intrigue. "Betty and I, you see, have the greatest desire to see all that is interesting in any place that we happen to visit, and if we were to have Gunther foisted off on us, it would cut down upon our pleasures vastly. We would never get to see Astley's Amphitheatre, because it would be quite *vulgar*, or the Elgin Marbles, because they are *indecent*, or, oh, any of a hundred things, and Gunther would complain because his feet hurt from tramping through old cathedrals for hours on end, or that the hackney was trying to cheat us of a few shillings—all perfectly ridiculous, you understand, or you would if you knew Gunther," Miss Hardy added.

"Yes, yes, I suppose I would," the duke murmured thoughtfully.

"So, you see, it is much simpler if we contrive to slip away—if Papa thinks that we are out visiting some fashionable modiste, or at some very dull tea, or something of that nature," Miss Hardy concluded complacently. "Papa can have some amazingly Gothic notions about propriety."

"I see," the duke said, and wondered. Like many shy people, Cordelia seemed to have developed a will of her own. "But I can see where your father would not approve of your jauntering about in a hackney coach. It just isn't done!" he felt forced to add.

"Not done, your grace?" Miss Hardy asked. "But it is the way in which we have accustomed ourselves to doing it in every city we have visited, you know. Surely, your grace, thousands of persons must visit the city every year and see it in just such a manner."

He was almost certain that he was being quizzed, and was not at all sure that he liked the experience. After all, no one quizzed the Duke of Overslate! "But, Miss Hardy!" he remonstrated, unconsciously adapting the same tone he might have used with his younger sister. "Young ladies who wish to establish themselves in London society do not allow themselves to be seen going about in hackney coaches! Not unless they wish to be considered fast—and I am sure that you do not wish to be considered fast."

Cordelia's lips tightened, and she turned her large brown eyes upon him with the utmost seriousness. "Your grace," she said in a low voice, "if you do not think my position in society is already irregular, not to say dubious, then you are more naive than I suspect you to be! Again, I do not care for society, any more than society cares for me." Scarlet-faced, she returned to her plate, and the duke was left staring at her profile.

Harry was somewhat stunned to find himself thus given a setdown, when he had merely tried to be helpful, and from such a source. For a moment, he suspected her of being coy, and then, realizing how impertinent what he had said must have sounded to her, coming, as it surely had, on top of what he suspected had been certain snubs she had already received from members of his class, he recognized his own lack of tact. Miss Hardy seemed impressed neither with his rank nor with that milieu in which he moved, when, by his own expectations, she should have been fawning all over him. That she did not find the ninth Duke of Overslate a person in whom she must stand in awe was a novelty for him, and to his own amazement, he was even further intrigued.

Unfortunately, at the moment he wished to proffer her his apology, the veal was removed in favor of the beef course, and his manners forced him to turn his attention toward his cousin.

Neither by word nor by gesture, both mediums by which Susannah was capable of conveying entire volumes, did she solicit the duke's opinion of the nabob and his heiress daughter, nor did she solicit his opinion in that same subtle language. Instead, she launched into a deceptively commonplace topic. "You know, Harry, I had a letter from your sister Dorothea in Bath," she said calmly, regarding him with her blue eyes. "She has requested me to send her a pair of London gloves for her first Bath Assembly."

"No," Harry said, "I did not know. But surely, at her age—"

"Dorothea is quite of an age to attend a Bath Assembly, Harry," Susannah continued blandly, sipping her wine. "And since she intends to go with her schoolfriend Miss Wimpole, chaperoned by Miss Wimpole's mama, I can see no objection to the plan. It will give her a little polish before she makes her London debut."

"Yes," Harry admitted, feeling the first thrust of his cousin's sword, disguised beneath those bland words.

"I *thought* you might," Mrs. Southbie agreed smoothly, and this time allowed herself to give her cousin a very meaningful look. "And I also had a letter last week from Victor—your brother—requesting the wherewithal to purchase a hunting spaniel pup. I didn't think that one had time to hunt at Harrow—at least my brothers never did. But it *did* put me in mind that he will be entering Cambridge next year," she added, and her meaning was clear to Harry.

If he was a little stung that his brother and sister should apply to their beloved cousin rather than to himself for the means with which to purchase their fripperies, it did serve to remind him that he was, at best, an indifferent correspondent, and that as the twins approached their maturity, they would be placing a further drain upon his resources. Susannah's shaft had found its mark.

"Their allowances," Harry managed to say, "should be sufficient to get them from one quarterday to the next without having to apply to you, Susannah." But he had received the message to think not of himself, but of them, and he had to content himself with that,

34

despite a sudden yearning to box Susannah's ears for achieving that brilliant piece of subtle strategy.

It would have been less than truthful to say that the duke was not relieved when the withdrawal of the ladies followed the removal of the last of the *sorbets, gateaux,* and fruits, leaving the gentlemen for the port and cigarillos. Harry was beginning to think that he was a dismal failure at the practiced art of gallantry. Each conversational gambit he had attempted to open with Miss Hardy had been met with a monosyllabic rebuff, leaving them both to struggle through the food in awkward silence. Miss Hardy, regretting her outburst, lapsed back into silence lest she compound her mistake, and Harry, wracking his brains for some sally or *bon mot* that would be both charming and gallant, cursed himself for an oaf. It was a hard time for them both.

But the withdrawal of the ladies from the board led to an interminable period of port, tobacco smoke, and such talk of business and politics between his cousin and Mr. Hardy that Harry very soon was able to think that Miss Hardy's silence was preferable to her father's opinions.

Hardy, it seemed to the duke, lost no chance to talk of his own vast fortunes, nor the opportunities to be seized by any young man of wit and cunning who might chance to venture into the New World.

He could and did expound at great length upon the various stratagems which he had employed to bring himself to his present pinnacle of success, and frequently contrasted his own adventuresome spirit with that of his contemporaries, who had preferred to remain at home in England, resting insecurely upon their ancient laurels, looking down upon the world of commerce as something intolerable.

When at last Harry had heard enough, he ventured to ask Mr. Hardy why his adopted country had turned upon the motherland at the height of the French threat, biting the hand that fed them. He was met with two pairs of blank stares.

"Well, your grace," Mr. Hardy said at last, frowning at him from beneath his bushy brows, "it's plain to see that you're as naive as a babe unborn in these matters. It's not who's right or wrong, but I tell you, the Americans were right enough in what they did."

"Let me tell you," Harry said, pushed to the end of his tether, "we could have used those troops in Spain, right enough, rather than sending them halfway around the world to fight—"

Mr. Southbie cleared his throat warningly, and Harry, recalling himself, lapsed into a sullen silence. But it was clear to him that Augustus Hardy, the mere second son of an insignificant country baronet, looked down upon the Duke of Overslate as if he were another piece of merchandise to be bought or sold as the occasion demanded, and a loathing for the man surged up from within Harry's breast.

"Think we ought to join the ladies," Beau suggested blandly, rising from the table.

But another surprise awaited the duke when the three gentlemen trooped into the blue salon, where the impassioned interpretation of a Mozart sonata cascaded from the pianoforte.

At first, the duke assumed that the musician was Miss Featherstone, for pianoforte was one of that lady's many educational talents, but he soon realized that Miss Featherstone could never play with such fire.

Indeed, that lady had settled her formidable puce bulk into a chair opposite Mrs. Southbie, who was presiding over the sherry and the cups at a low table before the hearth.

The musician was none other than Miss Cordelia Hardy. With a calm assurance, her fingers rippled over the keyboard, coaxing such sounds out of the expensive rosewood instrument as had never been heard in that house.

Harry paused in the doorway, momentarily arrested by the transcendence of that lady as she played. She seemed to have been illuminated from within. Wrapped in her music, her face had taken on a character and expression of such loveliness that he was forced to blink once or twice in order to assure himself that it was indeed the innocuous Miss Hardy who sat before the pianoforte, seemingly possessed by her music.

The illusion, if illusion it was, lasted but a second, for as the duke stood transfixed by the lady and her playing, Hardy, standing beside him and nodding with satisfaction, leaned over and spoke into the duke's ear. "I was never one to care much for music m'self, your grace, but I made certain that my Cordy had the best masters that money could buy! Had a Frenchman teach her—an old aristo, come from the Revolution in Paris. She also speaks French and Italian with tolerable proficiency, and sings a little."

The duke, forced to acknowledge this speech, bowed coolly, and as Mr. Hardy's eyes met his, once again had the sensation that he was being sized up.

With a final trill, Miss Hardy finished her piece, slumping slightly in her seat, as if all the force had been drained from her by the energy she had placed into her music. But when she rose from the pianoforte and recognized her audience, her shyness bubbled up from within her, her face turned scarlet, and she made a stiff, self-conscious curtsy, her fingers gripping the sheet music with enough force to wrinkle the pages.

"Excellent! Excellent, my dear!" Mr. Hardy boomed, clearly proud of his daughter's accomplishments, understanding, Harry thought, absolutely nothing of her particular genius. "Perhaps you would give us that pretty little sonata you always play at home!"

Miss Hardy hung her head, her side curls hiding her cheeks. "Papa, I am sure that no one wishes to be bored to tears by my poor playing—"

"On the contrary, dear Cordelia," Susannah said kindly, "nothing could give us more pleasure, I assure you! My pianoforte has never been put to better use, my love! Please, honor us with another sonata!"

"Yes, indeed—you must!" Beau commanded. "Overslate will turn the pages for you, won't you, old man?"

From beneath her side curls, Cordelia's dark eyes met Harry's for a second, and he smiled encouragingly. Page turning for young ladies had not previously been one of his accomplishments, but if it meant further music from such a talented performer, he was willing to do his duty. With his encouraging smile, he stepped forward to take his place at the pianoforte.

Cordelia hesitated for a moment, then seated herself again at the instrument, selecting the music book and opening it to the proper page. She could have played the piece through forward and backward without the music, but somehow she did not feel that it was necessary to inform the duke of this small fact. She drew in her breath, flexed her fingers in her lap, and closed her eyes.

From his position, Harry watched in fascination as her face was transformed, and her fingers hovered over the keyboard before striking the first note. Suddenly she launched into the difficult piece, one of the new compositions from the German composer Beethoven, interpreting it with a fire that surely would have pleased the gentleman, had he been present. It pleased Harry, who was very fond of music, and had to recall himself from his reverie more than once to turn the page. He felt as if he had turned over a rock in the woods and discovered a diamond, and he studied Miss Hardy with a growing interest.

It was over all too soon for his taste, and Miss Hardy, having done her little performance, seemed grateful to retreat from the cynosure of the company to a chair beside Susannah. She seemed content to sit there, those remarkable fingers entwined in her lap, her reticule seemingly a source of fascination for her as the conversation moved over her head.

Miss Featherstone, under the guise of passing the cups, took the opportunity to inform the duke of the opinion of the household, namely that he would be a very great fool to pass upon this last chance. Harry, who was used to a lifetime of Miss Featherstone's opinions, was hard pressed to hold his tongue between his lips. "Depend upon it, your grace, you would be a fool to cast this aside!" she finished with an admonishing finger in his direction, nodding vehemently.

Susannah glanced up, and her eyes danced with mischief. Harry, ordinarily very fond of her rather wicked sense of humor, did not return her smile, and, indeed, was seriously tempted to give her a speaking look, until he realized that Miss Featherstone was speaking for her old charge.

Mr. Hardy was, at that point, monopolizing the general flow of the conversation with several very dull political theories about his adopted country's noble experiment in democracy, which inevitably led Beau into his own anecdotes about his parliamentary career. Susannah, who was accounted to be one of the foremost political hostesses of her party, soon voiced her own opinions upon political philosophy, and soon the air was thick with talk of Corn Laws and Reform, Talleyrand and Burr, and a great deal more that was guaranteed to bore Harry into a stupor, for his interest in such matters was, at best, minimal.

Every attempt by Susannah to draw either the duke or Miss Hardy into the general flow of the conversation failed utterly, for Harry expressed an undisguised boredom, and Miss Hardy seemed to have no opinions at all.

From time to time, however, their eyes met across the room, and they smiled at each other hesitantly before one or the other dropped the gaze.

It was some moments before Harry summoned the courage to do what he would have naturally and easily done under any other circumstances, and placed himself in a chair closer to Miss Hardy. Two pink spots appeared in her cheeks as he seated himself beside her, but she looked up and smiled with what he fancied was a grateful look. Now what? he wondered. How did one engage in a light flirtation? Never was there a more awkward situation! Overslate, who had faced down the cannons of Waterloo, tongue-tied before a shy female in his cousin's drawing room. He smiled, and Miss Hardy smiled in return. Her heart was pounding against her ribs, pleased that he was sitting by her while the endless debate raged above their heads.

"You play very well, very well indeed!" Harry finally managed to say.

"Thank you," Miss Hardy replied, pleased, for she met his gaze with a little smile.

"No, really, you do," Harry said. He pushed a hand through his hair, and plunged onward. "I hope that I did not offend you at the dinner table. It was rude of me to pretend to know what you should do to go on."

She shook her head. "No, I am—as prickly as a porcupine of late! It—it was very kind of you to want to tell me—to give me a hint about how I should go on! But I must warn you that I shall not change my plans one iota to please society. Since I am not a member of that group," she added stiffly.

He nodded, at a loss for what to say next.

Harry studied her profile for a second, frowning with concentration. He was not doing well, he thought, not well at all. A more practiced man would have had Miss Hardy laughing and talking by now, perhaps slapping her fan against his knuckles. Any lady who could play with such gusto and passion clearly hid a great deal beneath that placid surface, he thought. If only he knew how to draw her out!

At that moment, Susannah announced that there would be fruit and cheese, and the heated political discussion broke up, the company moving into smaller circles. Miss Featherstone claimed Cordelia's attention with a question about her French music master, and Susannah took the opportunity to draw Harry aside under the pretense of examining Miss Hardy's music.

"Well, dear Harry!" Susannah breathed calmly, flipping through the pages. "I hope that my efforts have not gone unrewarded tonight!"

"Susannah, you are a conniving, interfering female! You run Beau's career mercilessly, you manipulate your party, and now you are attempting to manipulate me!" Harry said dangerously.

Susannah smiled complacently. "Yes, I am dreadful, am I not?" she answered in a composed tone of voice. "I think you had better marry solely so that you will escape my Machiavellian intrigues!" In spite of herself, she allowed a little gurgle of laughter to bubble from her lips, and Harry shook his head. "Miss Hardy will not keep you beneath the cat's paw, after all, and after years of having me ruthlessly thrusting heiresses beneath your nose, think how peaceful it will be to settle down with a lady who is possessed not only of an immense fortune but of a good, quiet nature! It will be so peaceful for you, Harry!"

"I don't see that I have choice in the matter," Harry

said glumly. "But, good Lord, Susannah, the father—"

Mrs. Southbie turned to look at him. "Beau and I," she said steadily, "are very fond of Mr. Hardy. He is amazingly droll. I've never known you to be a high stickler before, Harry. Beggars cannot be choosers."

"But I've never *married* before, either," Harry pointed out. "The persons one chooses for friends and the persons one chooses to connect onself with are two entirely different matters! To have him as a father-in-law would be far worse than having you married to my cousin, if you wish to talk about *interfering—*"

Susannah lifted one elegant shoulder. "Mr. Hardy wishes to establish his daughter in the peerage so that he may go back to America and boast of the matter. I assure you, once the thing is done, Harry, he will be on the next ship across the Atlantic. His aspirations are not for himself, but for dear Cordelia—and I need not tell you that our aspirations are for you. Consider what is due to you as head of the family, Overslate!"

Harry recognized the truth of this matter. Marriages of convenience were commonplace in the circles in which he and his cousins had been born, and he recognized this *mésalliance,* however difficult, might be the way out of his difficulties. And, yes, he was intrigued by Miss Hardy, and wanted to get to know her better. "This is all very well," he finally admitted grudgingly, "but how the devil does one go about courting heiresses, after all?"

Susannah smiled. "Like any other female. You speak to her father and ask if you may call upon him to ask his permission to pay court to his daughter."

"Of course," Harry agreed impatiently. "I know *that.* The thing of it is, I'm no hand at paying court to anyone, Susannah! Not in the petticoat line at all!"

"You'll learn, my dear Harry, you'll learn. But I think you should go and have a word with Mr. Hardy. He's rather expecting it, you know," she returned complacently.

Harry looked down at Mrs. Southbie, his expression stunned. "I wonder that Beau has not strangled you

41

long ago!" he finally said. "You are the most *managing* female of my relations!"

Mrs. Southbie nodded complacently. "Oh, I know that I am, Harry! My mother-in-law is forever reminding me of that fact! Someone has to do it—the Chrisfields are such an astonishingly *lazy* tribe when it comes to these things." She smiled over his shoulder and gave out her hand. "Ah, Mr. Hardy! I am so glad that you could spare us your presence tonight, and bring dear Cordelia with you. I think that Overslate would like to have a word with you."

"My pleasure, Mrs. Southbie, my pleasure!" Mr. Hardy boomed genially, bending gallantly over her hand with a twinkle in his eyes.

"You are too kind, sir," Susannah murmured with a wicked look at her cousin. "I see that Cordelia might need another cup! If you gentlemen will excuse me..." With a rustle of skirts, she drifted away.

Mr. Hardy glared upward at the duke from beneath his remarkably bushy brows, linking his hands behind his back. "Well, sir?" he asked.

For a moment, Harry was sure that he could not go through with it. But he thought of Overslate Castle's need for new roof, of the faces of his creditors, and of the future of his brother and sister, and he swallowed his pride.

When at last he took his leave of the Southbies and was out upon the streets again, he summoned a linkboy to guide him through the dark streets. It seemed fairly clear to him that like it or not, he was suing for the hand of the little American nobody.

He squared his shoulders, inhaling deeply of the foggy London night, wondering to what lengths he must go to preserve Overslate and secure the future of the Family. "To Waitier's, my lad, and don't spare the horses!"

The linkboy looked at him strangely. Truly, the lad thought, the toffs were an odd lot, and no mistaking the matter, none at all!

CHAPTER THREE

"A proper English breakfast, there's nothing quite like it," Mr. Hardy said in tones of the greatest satisfaction as he pushed himself away from the table and observed the ruins of his meal. Ample platters of ham, kidney, kippers, eggs, bacon, muffins, and toast had all been sampled, and washed down with some of his own East India coffee brew. The buttons on this day's waistcoat, a splendid affair of teal-blue silk brocade embroidered in silver thread, strained dangerously across his wide stomach as he fished in his pocket to consult his watch.

Miss Cordelia Hardy, a more delicate appetite, sipped at her coffee and merely nodded, wondering, not for the first time, what genius of perversity could seize an entire nation that they must roast their bread upon the fire and then allow it to arrive tepidly at the table, crumbling to the touch, and call the matter *toast*.

It was simply another one of the cultural riddles that contrasted England and America in her mind. How could two nations be so similar in so many ways, and so opposite in so many others?

Only consider last evening at the Southbies'. In general, she had always felt comfortable in the company of that couple, much more so than with any of her father's other friends, or so-called friends. But last night, she had sensed some sort of peculiar strain upon the gathering. Perhaps it had been the presence of Overslate.

Unbeknownst to herself, a faint smile lifted the corners of her lips when she thought upon the duke, only to fade away again.

Experience had long ago taught her that it was foolish to place too much faith in the careless promises of gentlemen who found themselves in her company, particularly in what they must consider very dull gatherings. Doubtless by this morning Overslate had forgotten all about his attempt to make conversation with Miss Hardy. Cordelia was all too well aware that her shyness made her less than the sort of lightly flirtatious, gaily charming dinner partner most relished by gentlemen such as the Duke of Overslate. All too frequently, after such evenings, she had lain awake, allowing the remarks and replies she *should* have made to rise in the sleepless watches of her mind, castigating herself for her own reticence.

"And tell me, Cordy," Mr. Hardy said suddenly, as if he had been reading her thoughts, "what did you think of last night's dinner at the Southbies'?"

Cordelia directed a level glance at her father, torn between exasperation at his perpetual hopefulness and her daughterly fondness for his gruff, generous heart. When, she wondered, would Papa ever give up hope that some knight in shining armor would arrive to rescue her from her maiden state? Carefully, she sipped at her coffee before replying. "I thought Mrs. Southbie everything that a charming hostess should be," she replied diplomatically.

Mr. Hardy's brows twitched up and down. It never failed to amaze his daughter that a man who could be so shrewd in business could be so blind to the nuances of social interaction beneath his very nose. It was as if he were deliberately blinding himself to the fact that she was a mere drab of a female, and not the sort of

44

gay, dashing lady that gentlemen like Overslate were likely to find irresistible.

Mr. Hardy pushed his lips in and out. "And what did you think of Overslate?" he asked a trifle impatiently, hooking his thumbs into the pockets of his vest and regarding her closely.

Although this was a question that Cordelia had been turning over in her mind for a greater part of last evening and this morning, she merely lifted her shoulders slightly. "I thought him most civil," was all that she replied, however, addressing herself to crumbling a piece of dry toast between her fingers.

This reply seemed to satisfy her father somewhat, for it seemed to her that a rather odd look of relief crossed his features, and he looked thoughtful. "Civil," he replied, turning this over in his mind. "A bit high in the instep, of course, but that's the way these dukes are. He has an enormous house in the country—quite a showplace it is, you know. The Chrisfields are one of England's oldest families—most distinguished, after all, although they're up the drainpipe, like many of them. I noted that you two seemed to go on well enough last night," he added hopefully.

"The duke was most civil," Cordelia replied again.

"Civil? He's promised to call upon us. I'd say that was more than just civil, Cordy."

Mr. Hardy was clearly fishing, his daughter knew, and in spite of herself, she shook her head slightly. Not for the world would she disabuse her papa of the notion that Overslate was vastly taken with his daughter. It gave him an enormous amount of pleasure, after all, and he would find out soon enough that the duke had only been making polite, empty promises.

As if to distract herself, she picked up the sheaf of the morning's post, quickly thumbing through the missives that had been left by her plate by the major-domo.

"Any invitations? I understand from Lady Armthea that Mrs. Knight is giving a grand ball on the twenty-third," Mr. Hardy said.

"No invitations, Papa," Cordelia replied. "Just some dressmakers' bills and an advertisement for a hair restorer."

Mr. Hardy tried to conceal his disappointment by running his hand over his bald pate and suggesting ruefully that perhaps he ought to send Shadwell out in search of this miraculous product. "Well, perhaps it will arrive tomorrow. I did make myself recalled to her at the opera the other night, after all," he said, and Cordelia, recalling Mrs. Knight's rather chilly reception of this old acquaintance reclaimed, merely nodded.

There was a brief silence as Cordelia studied the bills, for she was scrupulous in keeping her own accounts straight, and Mr. Hardy drummed his fingers upon the table.

"Cordy," he said at last, clearing his throat, "there is something that I ought to tell you, my girl. I have been waiting for the right moment, but..."

Cordelia's brown eyes met her father's and read the discomfort reflected therein. "What is it, Papa?" she asked gently.

Mr. Hardy cleared his throat, spreading his thick fingers on the cloth and regarding his daughter from beneath his eyebrows. "The thing of it is, Cordy...well! You know that you will be a great heiress one of these days—that you have a great deal of money, and..."

"Yes, Papa?" Cordelia asked when he had paused for some moments, obviously floundering about in search of the proper words. "Is there something wrong with my investments?"

Mr. Hardy shook his head again, this time vehemently. "Nothing of the sort! Everything's as right and tight as it can be, now that Boney's on St. Helena! Business has never been better! It's about—about your future!"

"My future, Papa?" Cordelia asked, curious, but not alarmed.

Mr. Hardy nodded uncomfortably. "Well, yes. Something has to be done about your future, you know," he began, then changed his direction. "Mrs. Southbie and I have put our heads together and thought a great deal about it, you see. You know, Cordy, that I want to see you well established, and that Mrs. Southbie is very well connected...."

"Susannah is my friend. One of the few genuine

friends I have made in London," Cordelia countered, wondering what her father was getting at.

"Exactly so! And, like me, she has your welfare at heart," Mr. Hardy said. "That's why—"

"Excuse me, sir. Oh! Good morning, Miss Cordelia! Do I interrupt?" Gunther Shadwell, Mr. Hardy's secretary, scraped upon the door with his fingernails, a toothy smile flashing across his countenance. Mr. Shadwell, fully six feet tall, with a long, gangling body, resembled, in Cordelia's opinion, nothing so much as a spider. His arms and legs always seemed to be moving at contrary angles, and his face, half masked behind a pair of extremely thick spectacles, resembled that of a member of the arachnid family, with his pasty complexion and large teeth. An unfortunately long neck, up and down which his Adam's apple bobbed at an alarming rate when he was nervous, which was a great deal of the time, only enhanced this impression, while his habit of speaking in a husky, somewhat mannered voice never failed to produce the impression that he was acting in an extremely bad play.

"Well, what is it, Shadwell?" Mr. Hardy almost roared in his irritation at having his little speech to his daughter thus interrupted.

Mr. Shadwell, oblivious of the contempt in which his employer seemed to hold him, bobbed several times, rustling a sheaf of papers in his hands. "It is these foreigners, sir! I cannot help but feel that they cannot be trusted to deal with us accurately. Clarke and Younge's invoices show that there is some seventeen shillings a hogshead difference between the price they agreed upon and the price they are billing us for, sir." He shook his head sadly. "It is not at all what one is used to in America," he added.

"Hellfire!" Mr. Hardy muttered, casting his napkin down upon the table. "Let me see that!"

Cordelia, aware of Shadwell's rather beady eyes upon her, rose from her chair. "I can see that you will be occupied with business, Papa."

Mr. Hardy, somewhat relieved by this timely distraction from what might have become a highly delicate discussion, nodded. "Yes! We shall finish this little talk some other time. What do you do today, daughter?"

Miss Hardy held her breath for a second. "Oh, I believe that I am to attend a—a balloon ascension!" she said quickly. "Do not expect me for lunch—Betty and I shall be gone until late afternoon."

"Teatime, then?" Mr. Hardy said, and his daughter nodded. "Very well, off with you, my dear, and enjoy yourself. Should you require funds?" he inquired, patting his pocket.

Cordelia shook her head. "Oh, no! I am quite certain that I am very plump of pocket, thank you! If you will excuse me—good day, Shadwell," she added, brushing past the secretary swiftly.

"Miss Cordelia!" Shadwell said almost reverently, staring after her as she made her way out of the study and down the hallway toward her own suite.

"Shadwell!" Mr. Hardy snapped.

The secretary recalled himself. "Oh, oh, yes sir. These invoices..."

Some twenty minutes later, Betty, the stout countrywoman who served as Miss Hardy's maid, opened the door of her mistress's suite and peered about the hallway. "'S clear, miss," she said, slipping out the door and stepping aside to allow her mistress to pass.

Miss Cordelia Hardy, attired in a bottle-green walking dress of merino, with slashed sleeves and copper-colored frogging, her gloved hands still lacing her bonnet beneath her chin, emerged into the hallway. "Do you have the guidebook?" she asked.

"Right here in my pocket. And the doorman's got us a hackney waiting," the maid replied, nodding.

"Good," Cordelia said, and together the two females made as if to steal toward the stairs, beating a hasty retreat.

"Miss Cordelia!"

Mistress and maid exchanged a significant look as Gunther Shadwell emerged from a recession in the wall, loping toward them with his spiderish stride.

Cordelia sighed. "Yes, Gunther?" she asked, a trifle impatiently.

Mr. Shadwell, oblivious to the subtle annoyance in

48

Miss Hardy's voice, leaned across the banister. "If I might have word with you?" he breathed, exposing his teeth in an obsequious smile.

"What is it, Shadwell? I am in a bit of a hurry," Cordelia said in the tone she might have used to address a slow child.

"A word with you—in private," Shadwell said significantly, looking at Betty.

"There's nothing the likes of you can't say before me," that woman insisted immediately, bristling at her old enemy. "Me, that's been with miss since her mother's days, and poor miss before that," she added cryptically, as if ready to defend her mistress with force, if need be.

"I'll thank you to remember that you are a servant, Betty!" Mr. Shadwell hissed, losing his composure slightly.

"Yes, and my most loyal friend," Cordelia added gently. "What do you wish to say, Gunther?"

It was obvious that the secretary did not relish stating his business upon the stairwell, but since Cordelia had no intention of making herself private with him, he had no other choice.

"It is only this, Miss Cordelia," he blurted out at last, with a sidelong glance at the protective Betty. "I am worried about you!"

Cordelia repressed a smile that rose to her lips. "Worried about me?" she asked, a little startled. "Whatever for?"

"As one who has always had your best interests at heart, Miss Cordelia," Shadwell said in histrionic tones, leaning across the rail to peer myopically at his employer's daughter, "I feel it is my duty to speak out! I cannot remain silent!"

"It always seems to be your duty to speak out," Betty commented sourly. "And I'd like to know who placed miss's best interests upon you."

Mr. Shadwell glared at the maid, and Cordelia was forced to bring her muff up before her lips, lest they betray her laughter.

"As one," Mr. Shadwell started again in self-important tones, "who has your best interests at heart, Miss

Cordelia, I feel that it is my duty to speak out! Here, among foreigners, we, who are used to a simpler, less treacherous life than that led in these alien parts, may fall into traps!"

Cordelia looked quite blank, and Shadwell, seeing that his pronouncement had fallen upon uncomprehending ears, plunged forward, only a little disconcerted. "I have noted, while others may remain oblivious," he said with a side glance at Betty, "that you have been going out a great deal! Staying up until all hours, arising once again in the morning to attend some function or another—it cannot help but have a deleterious effect upon your health, Miss Cordelia! I am also concerned about your association with persons, while perhaps of exalted rank and birth, who nourish the European treacheries within their breasts!"

"I beg your pardon?" Cordelia asked, completely bewildered by the hyperbole with which Mr. Shadwell invested the simplest statements.

"As one who wishes you well, I am concerned that your native American innocence will be trampled and crushed beneath the sophisticated mores of the Old World!" Mr. Shadwell declared passionately. "The toll that such socializing, and such association, can take upon your health and welfare disturbs me profoundly! I only speak as one who wishes you well!" Carried away by his own emotions, Shadwell took Miss Hardy's hand within his own and seemed about to press it against his breast, but as he threw back his head, the sight of his large Adam's apple bobbing up and down in his neck quite overset Cordelia, and she drew her hand quickly away from the secretary's grasp.

"Thank you, Shadwell," she said in a rather unsteady voice. "I appreciate your concern. But I assure you that I am quite able to handle myself without your assistance. I do have my father to look after me, you know, and I am certain that he would not allow me to move in disreputable company, even if I wished to do so!"

Gunther Shadwell shook his head. "But—but—Miss Cordelia! These foreign parts are not at all what one is used to! You cannot possibly understand—"

"Miss understands well enough, and having the likes of you bothering her head with your fidgety notions is not what I would wish to have to report to Mr. Hardy!" Betty said firmly, taking her mistress's arm and glaring upwards fiercely. "Bobbing-block! Take yourself away, you Paul Pry, before I pries you!"

And before Cordelia could protest, the sturdy maid was leading her down the stairs, still muttering under her breath.

"I am sure that Gunther means well," Cordelia said gently.

Mr. Shadwell, trembling with indignation at the way in which he had been routed again by the likes of Betty Malaone, stood at the head of the stairs, his thin lips pursed into an unpleasant expression. A more sensible individual might have been seriously deterred by Miss Hardy's obvious lack of interest in his suit, but sensibility was not among Gunther Shadwell's virtues. It was his single ambition in life to advance himself to the very top of his employer's vast empire, and he saw Miss Cordelia, and her fortune, as another step in securing his ambitions. In order to pay his court to her, he had undertaken this journey to the Old World, and it had been a hideous experience for him, since he was not a good traveler. All attempts to worm his way into Miss Hardy's affections had been met with severe rebuffs, but Shadwell was able to put this down to Miss Hardy's maidenly modesty rather than an aversion to his person. Since Mr. Hardy had not taken his secretary into his confidence regarding his ambitions for his only daughter, Shadwell had no way of knowing that his employer planned a far more noble future for her. But a lifelong habit of lingering at keyholes and doorways had led him to suspect that something was afoot, and he was determined that nothing should stand in the way of his plans.

"Shadwell! Damn the man!" Mr. Hardy's voice boomed from his suite, and with a little sigh, the secretary made his spiderlike way toward the study.

CHAPTER FOUR

The Duke of Overslate had passed a restless night, and its effects showed upon his countenance when he made his appearance in Mr. Hardy's suite that afternoon.

When the duke had arrived, that merchant prince had been seated behind his desk, illuminated from behind by a ray of sunshine, holding Harry's card in his hand, his brows drawn together, all the joviality of the previous evening gone from his aspect as he bade the duke to be seated and rose to his feet, grasping his hand in a bearish grasp.

Now, he was pacing the length of the carpet, his head down, his hands folded over his enormous waistcoat, regarding Harry from beneath his heavy brows, the complete man of business.

For his part, Harry felt trapped by the weight of the stare that had intimidated many a lesser man. He sat rigidly in his chair, returning the look with as much grace as he could muster, and suppressing an urge to lift his quizzing glass to his eye. It was necessary to remind himself that the fate of Overslate Castle hung in the balance.

"Well, it's a damned awkward situation, and no mistaking it!" Mr. Hardy exclaimed gruffly, pausing beside the window.

Harry made a pretense of examining his fingernails, wishing himself a thousand miles away. "It is not what I would have chosen," he agreed. "But I have come to ask your permission to pay my addresses to Miss Hardy."

"Nor is it what I would have chosen!" Mr. Hardy said a trifle mendaciously. "Your estates are shab-run, shab-run indeed, sir, and there is no getting around the fact that it will take a great deal of brass to set matters aright again—if I choose to do so!"

A muscle in the duke's jaw twitched, but he remained silent.

Mr. Hardy ran a hand over his bald pate, expelling a sigh. "But it's been the fondest dream of my life to see my Cordy set up as a peeress. She's been raised up from birth with nothing but the very best of everything. The best education, the best house, the best clothes, the best people—everything that money could buy, she's been given. Yes, it's been my dream to see her become a peeress, and not to put too fine a point upon it, I've got more than the means to spring the dibs!"

Harry found himself wondering how a man like Augustus Hardy could have produced a daughter as shy and pliable as Cordelia, who would acquiesce to this scheme without protest.

As if he had read Harry's thoughts, Mr. Hardy shook his head. "Or course, there's no telling what my Cordy will do," he continued. "She can be led but not driven, and I won't see her making a match that she can't abide, mind you, although she is a good obliging girl, and not prone to romantic fits and starts, like most females! Besides, Cordy knows that I have great expectations for her future, and when she marries, she'll be a warm woman in her own right, not to mention what I'll leave to her when I stick my spoon in the wall—"

"I hope that may not happen for some time, sir," the

duke put in uneasily, only to be answered with a wave of one of Mr. Hardy's giant paws.

"I won't have her played false, or mistreated, mind you!" Hardy continued dangerously. "After all, what I give, I can take away. But if Cordy takes to you, there will be no limit to my purse!"

The duke's lips tightened. "I am not in the habit of abusing females, sir!" Harry exclaimed with as much control as he could muster. "Besides," he could not help but add, "as you say, Miss Hardy may not take to me."

The merchant prince shook his head, dropping himself heavily into a chair. "She'll take to you if you allow her to do so, duke! You're a personable enough sort of a man, after all, and Mrs. Southbie seemed to feel that you and m'daughter would scrape together well enough!" He pursed his lips, and when he spoke again, his voice was confiding. "There's only one thing that I must tell you, duke," he began, and there was a distinct edge of discomfort in his tone. "My Cordy can be led but not driven. I could only wish she were a little more forthcoming, but there you have it, she takes after her mother, and for all of her shy ways, as I say, she could be led but not driven." Mr. Hardy rubbed his hands together with a dry noise and licked his teeth. "If she knew that Mrs. Southbie and I had put our heads together and reached this compromise, she might not much care for it. Now, you and I are men of the world, sir, and we know how these things are done, but Cordy's American-bred, and well, you see how it is! She expects to be treated with a certain delicacy! Yes, that's the word! Delicacy!"

It was as clear as mud to Harry, but he was anxious to have done with this interview and be upon his way. Nothing could have been more distasteful to him than discussing a marriage of convenience with this gruff nabob prince. "Exactly so!" he murmured.

Mr. Hardy nodded, clearly relieved by his mistaken belief that he had explained this difficult subject. "It's like this! She knows that I have always had high expectations for her, and she knows that she's been brought up to expect the best—the very best that there is. Of course, I've not yet found a way to broach the matter to her head-on, so to speak, but I've a fancy to see her a duchess, and I'm certain that if she is treated in the proper way, she'll have no objection to your suit."

"I shall do my best to pay my addresses to Miss Hardy with all due respect for her person," Harry promised a trifle dryly.

"Exactly so! I am glad that we understand one another, then!" Mr. Hardy said. "I need not scruple to inform you, duke, that a certain amount of tact is absolutely necessary. As I say, my Cordy can be led, but not—"

"—driven," the duke finished with a frosty little smile.

Mr. Hardy nodded, his heavy brows beetling as he glared suspiciously at the duke. "Exactly so! Well, she knows what's expected of her, and I don't suppose that she'll give you a moment's trouble, if you scruple to make yourself agreeable to her! I've kept Cordy close by me, after all, and she's not had that many suitors." He nodded once or twice.

"I shall do my best to make myself agreeable, as you say," Harry replied coldly.

Mr. Hardy leveled his gaze at the duke. "If you're what she wants, you're what she'll have," he said, rising as if to signal the interview was at a close and offering Harry one of his enormous beringed paws.

"Well, never you mind, duke! It's not something that you should worry your head about," he said somewhat cryptically to a puzzled Harry. "Just you instruct your man of business—what's his name—Lacey?—to come around and see me, and you concentrate upon doing your best for my daughter. I am certain that once you have gotten to know one another, there will be no obstacles of dislike."

"As you say, sir," Harry murmured, far too relieved to be spared any further time in Hardy's company to question too closely into the matters to which the other man had alluded.

Mr. Hardy, sanguine in his belief that his point had somehow been put across, grasped Harry's hand, nodding his massive head. It was to be a near-fatal mistake, but he was too relieved that the matter had been discussed at all to much care whether or not the duke had fully comprehended Cordelia's ignorance of the circumstances revolving about her marriage. Besides, he told himself, there would be time and enough later to lay the matter before his daughter and persuade her to see the virtues of aligning her fortunes to a duchess's crown, after she had had the chance to settle herself as to the duke's virtues as a husband.

Much to Harry's relief, he was escorted to the door, and the interview was at a close. It was unfortunate that he did not note the lean and shadowy presence of Gunther Shadwell lingering near the door. But Shadwell had noted the duke.

It was only, Shadwell reflected grimly, a very great shame that the doors of Claridge's were constructed in such a way as to preclude even the most assiduous listener from gleaning more than a snatched phrase or two.

But the seeds of his suspicion had been planted in his mind by this unlikely caller, and Shadwell was resolved that it would certainly be in his best interests to use his talents to glean further information about this unprecedented visit from a peer of the realm.

By the time Harry had emerged from the hotel into the afternoon sunlight, he felt very much like a man who has begun to feel the noose of Fate growing ever tighter about his neck. His interview with the merchant prince had not been calculated to set his mind at ease concerning his proposed alliance with Miss Hardy, and to discover that she was, as yet, wholly innocent of the motivations behind his courtship left him stunned. His only pleasure at that moment was in rehearsing, in his mind, exactly what he meant to say to his well-meaning cousin and his wife concerning his prospective father-in-law, and his preference for a term in the Fleet to such an unholy misalliance, and he was so preoccupied with this matter that he failed to note that he had stumbled, oblivious, into a small crowd gathering upon the walkway before the hotel, until his ears were assailed, for the second time that day, with the unmistakable accents of the American version of the king's English.

Shaking himself out of his own reverie, Harry found himself being jostled between a drayman and a butcher's boy, neither of whom seemed to be able to resist standing about to watch what Harry soon perceived to be some sort of an altercation between a grizzled cockney hack and a rotund middle-aged female. It was from this sturdy-looking creature that the unflagging accents of America emanated, and to the great enjoyment of the crowd, she was brandishing a large, serviceable umbrella beneath the jarvey's nose, demanding stridently to know if he wished her to give him a taste of his own.

"You do be tellin' 'im, missus!" called the butcher's boy in delighted accents, and the crowd jeered.

Harry was in no mood to be entertained, and was just about to adjure the lad to move out of the way for his betters when he saw two ladies descended from their carriage, haughtily skirting the foray with their noses in the air. Gaining the safety of the portals of Claridge's, they paused, and one sniffed to her companion, "Is that not the Hardy chit's abigail?"

"Indeed so!" her companion replied. "Trust an American to create a vulgar scene! Really! And they want to make themselves at home in our drawing rooms!"

It was then, to his utter horror, that Harry saw what he had missed before in this scene, and that was no one other than Cordelia Hardy herself, the plumes in her bonnet nodding as she tried to assert her person between the hackney driver and the American female. Unfortunately, her diminutive stature did not command respect from either party, but the sight of a well-dressed lady attempting to make peace between the driver and her maid seemed to be adding amusement to the scene for the interested spectators.

Cordelia, in the greatest anguish, was attempting to tug at the sleeve of her maid, without effect, for that woman merely begged her to stand clear, since she had promised Cordelia's late mama on her deathbed that she would look after Miss Cordy, and look after her she had, through thick and thin, and she would not fail her now.

To see Miss Hardy the object not only of vulgar amusement but as potential food for gossip was more than Harry could bear, and all of his resolutions upon the Hardy family were forgotten as he gathered together the full majesty of nine generations of ducal breeding and shouldered his way through the crowd to grasp Cordelia firmly by the arm.

She emitted a little gasp of astonishment and made to draw away, but looking up and perceiving that it was Harry come to her rescue, her expression changed entirely, and she relaxed within his grasp. "Oh, Overslate!" she breathed in tones of a maiden being rescued from a dragon, and Harry found himself strangely gratified by the novelty of being looked up to by a female who obviously considered him a knight in shining armor. "I have been *so* stupid! I came away this morning without any money at all, and now we must pay off the hack, but he will not let either one of us go upstairs to get it, because he is certain that we are going to cheat him and—oh, Overslate!"

It was but the matter of a few well-chosen words and the production of his purse for Harry to settle the matter, and if he was aware of the irony of having to settle the hackney fare of an heiress who could easily have bought and sold him, he said nothing of it, merely waving away the suddenly sniveling jarvey, who, seeing quality, was now respectfully tugging at his forelock and saying in an ingratiating voice that he only wanted what was due to him and how was he to know that these Americans would not try to cheat him, all the while bowing toward Harry.

"And so you shall have it, if you do not take yourself off!" Cordelia's maid exclaimed, waving her umbrella at him again. "Let this be a lesson to you that Americans are not liars nor cheats!" Betty said, determined to have the last word. The jehu looked very much as if he wanted to make some reply to this, but when Harry gave him a look that had made hardened Peninsular sergeants tremble in their boots, he thought better of it, scrambling up on his perch betaking himself away in a great haste.

"Oh, your grace, I know not how to thank you!" Cordelia exclaimed, laying a small gloved hand upon his sleeve and gazing up at him. "You were quite right — it was extremely foolish of me to be jauntering about the city in a hackney coach!"

"Be that as it may," Harry conceded, "it will not do for you to be standing in the middle of this crowd becoming the food of gossip for the vulgar, Miss Hardy! Come away with me, and we shall take a turn in my phaeton instantly!" Even as he spoke, he was swiftly leading Miss Hardy away, and she only had time to call over her shoulder to the astounded Betty that she would not be in to tea, as she was going with the Duke of Overslate.

Betty, who had been about to protest, suddenly smiled and nodded, regarding Harry with very much the same expression as her mistress.

"Well," she said to the gape-mouthed butcher's boy as she made her way into the hotel, "what are you looking at? Be on your way!"

Bolton, his grace's groom, had been in his master's service since the day he had thrown Lord Harry up upon his first pony, and in that time had never known him to break his own rule about taking females up in his phaeton. He was far too well trained to betray the least surprise concerning the scene he had just witnessed, or the fact that his master was now breaking that rule, but as he swung himself up behind on the rear perch and crossed his arms over his chest, he wished that it were, indeed, his place to remind the master what was due the dignity of the Duke of Overslate.

Cordelia was far too stunned by her recent ordeal and her miraculous rescue to protest the way in which Harry had ruthlessly commandeered her away from Claridge's, but finding herself suspended fully six feet above the ground in a precariously sprung sporting vehicle drawn by a pair of restless grays, she uttered no protest, only dug her hands deeper into her muff as Harry took the reins and eased the phaeton swiftly out into the heavy flow of London traffic, conscious only of a vast sense of relief to be removed from the scene of her embarrassment.

"I cannot thank you enough for rescuing me!" she finally managed to say when they were well under way. "In truth, I do not know what I would have done if you had not come along! To be sure, Papa would have heard of it, and he would have been exceedingly vexed with me for doing such a thing!"

"As well he should have been," Harry replied lightly, quite forgetting his dislike of Mr. Hardy for the moment, in his role of rescuer of maidens. "I hope in future, Miss Hardy, you will confine your sightseeing jaunts to the proper courses. Was it worth it all, then?"

"Oh, yes!" Cordelia sighed. "We saw St. Paul's, and the Royal Exchange, and oh, a great many things. I daresay you have seen all there is to see, and would be bored of a recounting, however," she added doubtfully, settling herself back against the squabs and beginning to enjoy this method of traveling very much as Harry negotiated between a lumbering mail coach and a brewery wagon with only inches to spare. "Suffice it to say that it was wonderful to be free of social obligations for an entire day. And," she could not help but add naively, "it also meant that I was able to take a turn in your phaeton! It is a most elegant vehicle, your grace, and your team is quite fine!"

"Do you like them, then?" Harry asked proudly. "They are my only real self-indulgence, I think. When I was neck-deep in mud and blood in Spain, I promised myself that *if* I came out of it alive, when I sold out, I should buy myself a good equipage to celebrate the fact that I survived."

"Very—dashing!" Cordelia managed to say as Harry took a sharp turn against one wheel and brought them out upon a major street. Without quite knowing how, he seemed to be driving them in the direction of the park.

"Should you like to take the reins when we reach the Row?" he asked generously, surprised at himself.

The plumes in Cordelia's bonnet shook in the negative. "Oh, no! That is, I would not know how! Papa never thought it right that I should learn. He was afraid that I would do myself an injury, you see." Was there the trace of a regretful sigh in her voice as she added,

"Papa sometimes is almost overprotective of me, I think. Besides, you do it so well!"

If the truth were to be told, Harry was considered the merest whipster, as any of his cronies in the Four-Horse Club would gleefully have informed her. But how was Cordelia to know of such matters? Harry, unused to his new role of rescuer, basking in the novelty of having his driving praised even by such an uncritical eye as Miss Hardy's, was inclined to think very well of his companion at that moment. Truly, here was a fetching sort of female, he thought. "If we were at Overslate, I could certainly teach you within a trice," he said at his most sanguine. "It would be an easy thing indeed."

Bolton, whose misogyny had been matched until today by his master's, could not help himself from falling into a coughing spell, and was rewarded with a very sharp look. But since they were turning into the park at that moment, Harry was far too preoccupied with taking his place in the throng of fashionable turnouts taking the air at the promenade hour to give much thought to his own unprecedented offer.

"I should like that very much," Cordelia said after a little thought. "Papa never would allow me such a thing, though, even though it is a skill I have always wanted to acquire. To have my own turnout would suit me very much, I think," she added wistfully.

"It would seem that your father is much concerned for your well-being," Harry ventured a little dryly, recalling very well his interview with that person.

Cordelia bit her lower lip. "Perhaps a little too much so. But it is always so with an only child, I suppose. How lucky you are to have a brother and a sister."

Since Harry had never considered Lord Victor and Lady Dorothea to be fortunate additions to his life, he was forced to laugh aloud. But he was fond enough of the twins to agree that they made his life a great deal more interesting, and a recounting of their more colorful exploits had the result of making Cordelia wonder that anyone could be so totally without fear, until Harry, not unnaturally, went into a description of his heart's love, Overslate Castle and its estates.

Cordelia had long ago learned the best method to cover her shyness was to pursue a conversation with only a few questions upon a subject which interested her companion, leaving that person free to discourse upon a favored subject, with the result that she had to do very little speaking, and only listen. Since she found it not at all difficult to listen to anything that the Duke of Overslate might care to say, she was treated to a discourse upon such subjects as mortmains and drainage ditches, Tudor architecture and the evils of enclosure, and it was a great deal to her credit that city-bred as she was, she struggled valiantly to assimilate all these various details that went into the management of a vast estate. Practice with persons of far less interest to her than the duke made her questions incisive and intelligent, and it was not too long before Harry began to think of Miss Hardy as being a very good conversationalist, once she was removed from the overpowering presence of her father.

So intent was the duke upon his discourses on modern agriculture that he failed to note the stares of several persons upon himself and his companion as they picked their way through the throng of vehicles making way around the park. Even as he was explaining to Miss Hardy systems of estate management and crop rotation, he was tipping his hat to an august pair of dowagers in a landaulet, who stared back at the duke and his companion, the American nobody, their polite frozen smiles turning to stares as they eagerly pressed their faces together in rapid speculation. A few short days ago, such an event would have filled Harry with rage and embarrassment, but then a few short days ago he never would have considered riding at the fashionable hour with a lady of no particular distinction in his phaeton. Today, he barely noted, for he had become quite intent upon his discourses on Overslate, and was warmed to oblivion by the interest of his companion.

For her part, Cordelia saw only Harry, and liked very much what she saw. If he was used to playing the role of rescuer, she was very much unused to being in need of rescue, and his timely appearance could only add to his virtue in her eyes. Since it had never occurred to her that she might have been saved from the cynosure of one crowd only to be subjected to that of another, she was oblivious to the speculation their appearance was drawing.

It took Susannah Southbie, upon a very fine chestnut, habited out in the prettiest of russet velvets, drawing up beside the phaeton to deliver a smart tap with her riding crop to divert their attention from one another.

"Rein in, my good man!" Susannah cried gaily. "Beau and I have been hailing you from across the park for these past few minutes! Say that you will not cut me dead, not when I have quite disgraced myself by *galloping* after you!"

Harry obediently brought his horses to a standstill, and Mrs. Southbie leaned over to take Cordelia's hand in her own. "That is much better! How do you do, Cordelia, my dear? That's a very fetching hat. I should make Beau take me to Paris so that I may buy new clothes! Well, Harry, what *were* you telling Cordelia that neither of you heard us calling you down?"

"You are impertinent, as always, Susannah," Harry said, the dressing-down he had prepared for his cousin that afternoon quite forgotten in the fine glow of subsequent events. "And I should think in your delicate condition, you would not be galloping!" he added, trying to frown.

Susannah threw back her head and laughed. "Delicate! Good God, Harry, I've never felt better in my life! Besides, Beau and I mean this one to grow up to be a horse-breeder!"

"The duke was telling me about Overslate, and it was not at all dull, Susannah," Cordelia said loyally.

A roguish look flickered into Susannah's merry eyes, but she contented herself with merely saying, "How interesting," and turning in her saddle. "And here comes my lord and master! Beau! I say! I've caught them!"

Mr. Southbie came riding up beside his wife, a vision of sartorial splendor in a corbeau-colored hacking jacket and a low-crowned beaver. His eyes flickered speculatively over the pair in the phaeton, but like his wife, he made no comment, merely greeting Miss Hardy and her cousin with his slow, ironic smile. As always, Beau was impeccable, but it seemed that he could not resist the chance to lean from his saddle and flick a mote of dust away from one gleaming boot. "Well done, old man," he murmured beneath his breath. "It will only take a little pressing of the point to bring the matter to a happy conclusion now."

The duke had been enjoying his afternoon's adventures with Cordelia to such an extent that he had quite forgotten that it was her fortune and not her person which he was supposed to be pursuing. This reminder of where his duty lay served rather effectively to cast a pall over his enjoyment of the lady's company, and it suddenly seemed to him that what had been a pleasure before had now become a burden. He looked at his cousin rather bleakly, and Beau returned his look with his usual impassive stare, unaware that his well-meaning encouragement had, in fact, engendered quite the opposite effect.

Susannah, oblivious to the dialogue between her cousin and her spouse, was doing her very best to warm her friend's affections toward the duke. "Just you take care," she was saying merrily, "for there's a very good reason why Harry don't take females up in his phaeton in general! He's afraid he will overturn them as well as himself, you know!"

Cordelia's eyes widened at this piece of information, and she could only murmur that she felt quite honored to have broken a precedent. "But," she could not resist adding loyally, "he is a very good driver, Susannah! Complete to a shade!"

Such a remark may have only earned her a smile from her friend, but she could not know that it had elevated her considerably in the eyes of the duke's groom, who had begun to think that perhaps this lady, for all of her Americanness, might do very well for his master.

But Harry had overheard, and his mood was not elevated by thus being shown to a disadvantage by his quick-witted cousin. "You were always impertinent, Susannah," he managed to say with only a very little indignation, and although he smiled, it did not quite reach his eyes. Harry straightened himself on the seat and took up the slackened reins between his fingers. "Sorry we can't stop here for a coze, but I fear that I have kept Miss Hardy away from her father for rather longer than I had thought, and no doubt she has other engagements."

Cordelia looked very much surprised at this, but said nothing as Harry tipped his hat to his cousins and spun the phaeton down the pathway, leaving the Southbies full of self-congratulations and satisfaction on the excellence of their scheme.

On the drive back to Claridge's, Harry had lapsed into a moody silence from which no drawing questions seemed to be able to rouse him, and if Cordelia felt a slight amount of trepidation about something she might have done to be the instrument of his silence, her fears were seemingly alleviated when he escorted her back to Mr. Hardy's floor in the hotel.

She had turned at the head of the stairs to offer him her thanks when he grasped her hand in his own and spoke abruptly, aware of the pressure of time. "Miss Hardy! Is there a place where we may be private for a moment?" he asked suddenly, and Cordelia inclined her head questioningly.

Cordelia looked at him for a moment. "I don't suppose," she said at last, "that there would be anyone in the morning room at this hour. Your grace?"

Harry followed her down the hallway to this chamber, a small room off the main suite engaged by Mr. Hardy. It was indeed deserted at that hour of the day. The grate was cold, and a thin twilight filtered through the curtains at the windows, casting a watery, grayish light over the room. "I think that we may be private here," Cordelia said, crossing the room in a rustle of skirts and tossing her bonnet carelessly on a chair. "Shall I ring for a fire?" She stopped, her hand on the bell pull, and looked at Harry questioningly.

The duke had closed the door behind himself, and now stood beside it, his hands thrust deep into his pockets, watching Miss Hardy across the room. "No need for that. This won't take very long." He frowned at himself, cursing his own lack of eloquence. "That is, don't wish to keep you from your engagements—your activities—for too long!" He swallowed. This was going to be harder than he had expected. The courage which had never failed him on the battlefield faltered in the face of a single female, and he faced Miss Hardy with far less courage than he had faced Napoleon.

That she was looking at him with a vaguely amused expression did nothing to relieve his anxieties. He cleared his throat. "Miss Hardy!" he barked.

"Your grace?" Cordelia asked, quite at sea by now.

Harry ran a finger around the inside of his stock, feeling distinctly tongue-tied. He drew a deep breath, summoned his courage, and plunged in again. "I have spoken to your father this afternoon, Miss Hardy, and he has—" Here he broke off, at a loss. "Good Lord," the duke confessed frankly, "this is difficult! Thing of it is, not used to giving flowery speeches. Never done it before, you know! Not much of a man for the ladies!"

Cordelia, having seated herself upon the striped sofa before the window, was totally at sea, but inclined to be helpful. "There is a trick that we shy people use, your grace, when we are at a loss for words. If you say what you need to say, without roundaboutation, in a few simple words, it is much easier. Besides," she added, with a little sympathetic smile, "I am not at all used to receiving flowery speeches, your grace."

"Ah," Harry said, nodding. He had removed his hat, and was now turning it about in his fingers. He frowned down at this object in his hand for a moment, then started again. "Miss Hardy! I have spoken to your father this afternoon, and he has given his consent to—to allowing me to pay my addresses."

"Pay your addresses?" Cordelia asked, more lost than ever, and quite wide-eyed with astonishment. Of all the things that the duke could have suggested, this had been the furthest thing from her mind, if not from her secret heart. She was stunned. "You are proposing marriage to me, your grace?" she managed to ask.

Harry was expecting almost anything but surprise on the part of Miss Hardy, and interpreted her reaction as coyness. He was aware of a sense of annoyance, for clearly something more was expected from him. Until this moment, Miss Hardy had seemed to him, if not precisely the female of his dreams, at least a good sensible girl with no scatterbrained ideas about sentiment and romance about her. It suddenly occurred to him that perhaps *all* females, no matter what the circumstances, expected some sort of wooing when they received a proposal of marriage, even if it was simply a *marriage of convenience*. Unfortunately, it did not occur to Harry, as inexperienced as he was in these matters, that Cordelia was simply overwhelmed with the suddenness and the surprise of his proposal. After all, he had been led by her father to believe that she was expecting it of him, and knew her duty.

"You are—proposing to me, your grace?" Cordelia repeated, unbelieving. She flushed, shaking her curls from side to side. "That is to say—*what* are you proposing to me?"

"Why, marriage, of course!" Harry blurted out, raising one eyebrow and looking at Miss Hardy as if he had suddenly discovered her to be slow-witted. "Why else would I go to speak to your father? Marriage. Yes! Askin' you to marry me, Miss Hardy," he added, his voice more gruff than he had intended.

Cordelia blinked. Slowly, she rose in a rustle of skirts, pressing her trembling hands together at her waist and crossing the room to stand by the window. "This is so—so unexpected. We have only just met," she murmured.

A thin thread of sweat was beginning to form along Harry's spine. Hang her, he thought sullenly. Did she have to come missish on him just now? She knew as well as he did that this was just a matter of form, an arrangement between the two of them. Did she expect him to babble all sorts of drivel? His ignorance of the female sex, he decided, was truly appalling. Perhaps, he thought, at this point he was supposed to hold her hand, or make some sort of display of affection. It was, he admitted to himself, not an unpleasant prospect, but it did make him feel rather like a hypocrite, under the circumstances. Slowly, he crossed the length of the room and took one of her hands within his own, looking down into her brown eyes. "I know that under ordinary circumstances, I should have waited, Miss Hardy—but time is of the essence! I think that we might suit, you know. That is, your father thinks that we might suit, and I hope that he is correct!" The duke frowned, feeling like a schoolboy forced to recite. "Miss Hardy, I'm sorry, but I am not at all good at sentimental little speeches. I'm a soldier, after all! And this moment is not all that I would wish it to be, but the sooner we arrive at an understanding, the better off we both shall be."

Miss Hardy peered into those gray eyes questioningly, wondering if perhaps the duke did not feel well, or if there might be some trace of insanity in his family. She felt that she either wanted to laugh or cry, and she was not totally certain which. But he must be perfectly sincere, for he told her that he had spoken with Papa, and that Papa had given his consent, so certainly he must! Her heart was pounding and her head swimming. Surely, she would awaken to find that this was a dream!

"I think—this is so sudden—did you feel as I felt from that very first evening?" Cordelia managed to stammer out, caught between her shyness and her overflowing emotion. She shook her head, smiling up at the duke. "I know that my feelings for you are perfectly sincere, your grace! Is this not strange! I never believed that you—that this would happen to me! So sudden! Papa will be so happy! I am so happy!" Her hands grasped the duke's within her own. "I, too, am not very good with words, but I hope that you will understand what is in my heart!" Cordelia managed to say at last.

Harry, a little embarrassed by this display of emotion, supposed that it was what females did, and that, with time, she would be restored to herself. "Thing of it is, I am certain that we may each offer the other a decent sort of arrangement," he offered.

"I hope so, your grace! Believe me, I shall try to do my very best for you," Cordelia breathed, still attempting to assimilate that this was happening to her. It was, well, precisely like a novel, but never in her wildest and most secret fantasies had she thought that it would happen to her. For her, it had been love at first sight with the duke, and to find that he loved her—it was almost more than she could bear. "And Papa approves!" she concluded aloud. "He has always been so protective! I never thought that he would, but of course you are a duke, and that must figure to him!"

"You would, of course, become Duchess of Overslate, Miss Hardy," Harry said dryly, as if she needed to be reminded of that fact. "And you do bring certain, er, considerations of your own into the match."

Cordelia nodded. "Oh, yes! I *should* become duchess, should I not?" she asked naively, then gave a little laugh. "Oh, I can see why Papa agreed to the match! I hope that he was not terribly, well, forthcoming with his ready—as he would say? He can be very droll about such things, you know, as his fortunes. That is—I know that he has a great deal of money and that you are not as well off." She shook her head. "I am becoming a sad rattle, but you must understand, that is his way."

Doing it too brown, Harry thought, but decided that he admired her pride, at least. "Yes, yes, of course," he agreed. "We shall both have what we want, shall we not? I shall endeavor to do my very best for you, to treat you to every consideration to which a Duchess of Overslate is entitled...."

Cordelia drew herself up to her full height and met his gaze. "And I shall do my very best to be a very good duchess!" she promised.

Harry drew a breath of relief. "Then we are settled?" he asked.

"Oh, yes!" Cordelia sighed.

Harry seeing her happiness, interpreted it to mean that she was overjoyed to be upon her way to being established as a duchess. If he had known that her joy rose from her mistaken belief that he was as smitten with her as she with him, his feelings might have been quite different. But to his bemusement, she was standing right below him, her eyes half closed, her lips parted, and her chin raised expectantly. Here at least, Harry needed no prompting, for he was never averse to kissing a likable female, and at that moment, Cordelia was almost pretty. Very gently, he placed his lips against her own.

For such a shy female, Cordelia responded with an

unexpected fervor, her arms snaking about his neck, at first hesitantly, and then with all the strength of an awakening passion. Harry, fired by her response, took her in his arms and drew her against him, marveling how well her small form seemed to conform to the contours of his own, how her lips tasted sweet against his mouth.

At last, his own fine sense of propriety recalled him to his senses, and he gently disengaged her from his embrace, smiling down at her in spite of himself, and feeling very much as if he had taken advantage of an innocent maiden. Virginal females had never been in his style, and he felt a hypocrite for the sensations that Miss Hardy seemed to be causing within him.

Very gracefully, Harry took Cordelia's hand within his own and raised it to his lips. "I shall call upon you on the morrow," he managed to say. "Now that we are agreed, your father and you will be coming to Overslate Castle."

"Overslate Castle? Oh, I should very much like to see your home," Cordelia murmured, still feeling a little breathless. "You love it so much...."

If the thought of the Hardys—or, more specifically, Mr. Augustus Hardy—setting foot in his beloved ancestral pile disturbed Harry somewhat, he did his best to conceal it. But it did have the effect of bringing him back to a realization of his unfortunate circumstances, and the smile he gave Cordelia was slightly cool. "Of course," he said in a rather businesslike tone. "It would only be the proper thing to do, you know. You will have to meet my family before we can announce our engagement."

Cordelia opened her eyes wide, feeling a sudden trepidation. "Your family? But I thought that Beau and Susannah were your family."

Harry smiled, this time a trifle condescendingly. "Oh, they are only a *part* of my family, you know! But you need not fear! It will only be a ceremonial occasion. As Duchess of Overslate, you will be expected to preside over a great many such functions, you know. Only a couple dozen of my very dreary relations for a fortnight, then we need only see them again at weddings, funerals, and christenings!"

"Oh," Cordelia said in a very small voice. "I see! I shall do my best for you."

"I am sure that you will," Harry replied blithely. Having grown up among such duties, he could not envision that such a prospect might throw Cordelia into dread. They were, after all, only his relations, and he was the head of the family.

As the sitting-room door opened and the duke took his leave, neither he nor Cordelia was aware of the spidery form of Gunther Shadwell lingering in the long shadows of the hallway.

CHAPTER FIVE

Augustus Hardy was seated before his dressing table in a voluminous robe of embroidered Chinese silk, the heavily worked flowers and oriental dragons playing across the fields of his vast stomach in heartfelt abandon. His valet, a thin middle-aged person of immense dignity, was struggling, without much success, to arrange his employer's cravat into the folds of his several chins.

When the knock came upon the door and Cordelia, without waiting for a summons, thrust her head through the portal, Mr. Hardy met his daughter's gaze in the mirror and dismissed his man, casting aside the *Financial Times* and turning heavily upon his chair to regard Cordelia from beneath his heavy brows.

"From your expression, Cordy, I would say that you have a very good piece of news for your old papa," he said, not without a certain hopeful note in his voice.

Cordelia, leaning against the door with a little sigh, turned the strings of her bonnet in her fingers. "Papa,

Overslate has proposed to me!" she announced breathlessly.

The old man nodded. "I thought that he might," he said complacently. "And, daughter, what did you say?"

"I said *yes, Papa!* Oh, I said *yes!* Overslate said that you had approved the match—" Cordelia broke off, laughing, and looked at her father. "You did, didn't you? Oh, Papa, please say yes! I am so happy!"

"I approved," Hardy said and nodded.

"Oh, Papa, the duke is so wonderful! He is such an English gentleman, so full of reserve and dignity, but at the same time, he feels just as he ought! Do you think that there is such a thing as love at first sight? For you know, that is how I felt when I saw him at the Southbies, and he said, Papa, that he felt it for me! Oh, he didn't precisely say that, for he is far too nice, and has a great deal of reserve, but I could feel it, Papa! I know that he feels the same way about me!"

Intoxicated with love, Cordelia was transformed from a shy mouselike creature into a young woman who was alive and almost beautiful in the raptures of her first love. Watching his beloved daughter, Augustus Hardy allowed a smile to turn up the corners of his mouth. Cordelia was his flesh, and he could deny her nothing. Never before in her life had Cordelia seemed happier to him. It gave him a warm feeling to see her thus, and he felt a faint nostalgia for her late mama, wishing that Liza could be here to see what he had wrought.

Cordelia, lost in a reverie of love, had sunk into a sofa. "Oh, Papa, I feel so—so strange. It must be love, what else could it be? He loves me, Papa! Someone loves me!"

Hardy nodded, watching her closely, a muscle in his jaw working thoughtfully. How, he wondered, could he deny his daughter her happiness? Overslate had everything that he had always wanted for his girl. Power, position, a title. How, he wondered, could he spoil his daughter's happiness by telling her that he had arranged this match for her? That what she believed was love was something he had cold-bloodedly arranged, a convenience of dollars and cents in exchange for the rank of duchess? It would destroy his daughter's happiness in the moment, and that was more than Augustus Hardy could bear. It was a simple omission, after all, and women, in his belief, were not meant to trouble their heads about matters of finance and settlements. Let his Cordy be happy, he decided, in that moment. She would be a duchess, and in time, she would see that the outlay of a sum of money made little difference in the long run of things. After all, such transactions occurred every day. If she fancied herself in love with the duke, so much the better for all concerned, to her father's way of thinking. A husband was just another purchase that Augustus Hardy could make for his daughter. And, he decided, as a finale to his elaborate self-justification, Cordy could be led but not driven. It was all for her own good.

It was only a very trivial thing, after all, a very small price to pay when his dreams of Cordelia's future were about to be fulfilled beyond his own expectations.

"Is it not wonderful, Papa?" Cordelia asked, and for Hardy, the moment for truth was lost. Perhaps it would arise again at a later date.

"Indeed," the old man replied, laying a heavy hand upon his offspring's. "It is precisely what I would wish for you—precisely what I wanted."

If Augustus Hardy was able to pass his evening bathed in the triumph of his ambition, the Duke of Overslate's emotions were far less sanguine that night.

Mrs. Southbie, very becomingly attired in a dinner dress of rose crepe de chine, was descending the stairs from the nursery floor, her mind given over to a strong feeling of maternal pride in her eldest son's mastery of his Collect, when these happy domestic thoughts were rudely interrupted by the sudden appearance of what gave every inclination of a disturbance upon her landing.

Harry, his dress in what she could only deplore as a very sad state of disarray, was in the act of ascending to the floor, closely followed by the butler, that elderly factotum, red-faced and out of breath, exuding disapproval from every pore as he attempted to prevent

Harry from gaining access to the upper regions of the house.

"Your grace!" Treedle huffed. *"If you please!* Mr. and Mrs. Southbie are dining out this evening! Allow me to show you to the morning room! Strong coffee! Send for your man! Upset Mrs. Southbie!" But all of his words were of no avail, and he paused, horrified, as he caught sight of his mistress poised above this interesting scene, clearly at a loss to determine its cause. "Madam!" Treedle implored her. "His grace insisted upon showing himself in, despite my protests—"

Harry leaned against the banister and looked upward at Susannah, a roguish smile suffusing his features. "Hullo, Susannah! Want a word with you!" he said in a slightly slurred voice.

With a light tread, Mrs. Southbie descended the stairs. "Harry! Are you to dine at the Amberfields' also? Beau would never think to tell *me!*" Mrs. Southbie said briskly, crossing the floor with her hands extended toward her cousin. "But you are not even dressed!"

"Damn the Amberfields," Harry suggested, brushing his coat with elaborate grace as he turned to look at Treedle. "Told you that it was all right! Family! Won't turn away a man who's sold his birthright for a mess of pottage, or whatever it is!"

Susannah had been studying her cousin closely, and now she drew back a step. "Why, Harry," she said without turning an eyelash, "I do believe that you are a trifle foxed!"

"Utterly cast away!" Harry announced, supporting himself against the wall and grinning at her cheerfully, until his expression began to crumble. "Got a right," he added in a darker voice.

Mrs. Southbie frowned. As long as she had known her husband's cousin, she had never seen him even the least cast away, even after a night of hard drinking. Clearly, something was amiss.

"That, madam, was the conclusion at which I arrived when his grace appeared," Treedle huffed. "I, of course, attempted to restrain him, but short of laying hands upon him, there was little that I could do! I did not think it would be proper to summon the footman to help me restrain his grace!" Clearly, the venerable retainer was in a state of outraged dignity. If the Duke of Overslate did not know what was due his consequence, it was plain that Treedle did.

"I am foxed," Harry confessed sheepishly. "But if you were me, you would be too, Treedle!"

"Your grace!" that person replied in frigid accents, deeply offended by the familiar tone with which the duke was addressing him.

"Thank you, Treedle," Mrs. Southbie said in pacifying tones. "I know that you could be counted upon. Whatever would I do without you!"

Slightly mollified, the butler nodded, squaring his shoulders most manfully. "Perhaps, madam, I should bring his grace some coffee—very strong!" he suggested.

"Always talks around me when he's miffed with me," Harry said.

Susannah ignored this comment. "Yes, Treedle, I think that would be the best thing. And you might tell John Coachman not to let the horses stand! We may be delayed a bit. Harry, you may not sit on the landing, you know. Someone is likely to trip over you!"

"Just resting," Harry replied dismally. "Oh, what have I done? I am foxed, Susannah! Been at my club all afternoon working quite hard at it!" He cradled his head in his hands.

"Hullo, what's all this rumpus?" Beau, emerging from his dressing room, a long strip of linen depending from one hand, looked down at his cousin. "Oh, it's you, Harry. You can't bother Susannah right now—we're going out to dinner. Besides, I have been trying to tie my cravat for the past half hour, and you know that I cannot achieve perfection when there's the least disturbance."

Harry laughed, then rather rudely expressed an opinion as to exactly how his cousin might best employ his cravat, recalling himself long enough to apologize to Mrs. Southbie before burying his head into his hands once more.

"I say, old man," Beau protested, mildly enough.

"I think, my love, that Harry is cast away," Susannah remarked.

Beau nodded. "So it would seem. Well, we can't have him cast away on the landing. Bad influence for the children. Better put him in the dressing room."

Together, the Southbies approached Beau's beloved cousin, but at that moment, the duke looked up at them from bleary gray eyes. "Perfectly all right!" he exclaimed. "I have saved the house of Chrisfield! Don't a man deserve to be drunk when he's saved his home, done his duty to the family, and sold his birthright for a mass of pottage? Or is it a mess?"

"Yes, I suppose so," Beau agreed. "Come, Harry, sit up!"

But the duke shook his head. "Congratulate me! You must congratulate me! I have done what you wanted me to do! Performed my duty! Asked Miss Hardy to marry me! She accepted!" He threw back his head and laughed. It was a distinctly hollow sound. "Was there ever a man happier than I?" he asked.

The Southbies exchanged glances. "That explains it," Beau said. "Never seen Harry in his cups before. Must have fed him drink down at his club to celebrate the occasion."

"Yes," Susannah agreed. "That must explain it all. Harry foxed is a most unusual sight, after all. Come on, old dear, let us get some coffee into you now. Harry?"

The duke looked at his cousins. "I am a trifle cast away," he confided. "Not at all like me."

CHAPTER SIX

The heavy mists that had blanketed the landscape since their departure from London had lifted slightly when their coach turned up the long winding drive that led to Overslate Castle, and Cordelia, anxiously peering out the window for what would be her first glimpse of her future home, drew in her breath. "How very romantic," she said as the ancient seat hove into sight.

"A vast, rotting old pile!" Mr. Hardy muttered, looking over her shoulder. "I shouldn't wonder that it would take a pretty penny to bring this back into line!"

Shrouded in mist, Overslate Castle squatted in its park, a vast gray stone edifice in decidedly shabby repair. Centuries of thick ivy clung to its cold walls, and its turreted towers, however Gothic they might have been, looked deplorably in need of masonry work. Without the sun to give a glow to the many-paned windows or to illuminate the heavy carved woodwork of the porticoes and sills, the rambling structure seemed cold and inhospitable indeed, even to Cordelia, who was prepared to love anything that meant so much to her beloved. When Mr. Hardy, who valued his comfort, grumbled that doubtless the place was as drafty as a barn and that the chimneys smoked, if he knew anything, she could not protest, but merely settled back into the luxurious squabs of her father's hired coach and tried not to give way to an attack of nerves upon the prospect of meeting her future husband's relations.

"I wish that the Southbies had been able to come with us," she said suddenly. "I shall not know how to go on without Susannah to chaperon me."

"It was damned unfortunate that Mrs. Southbie's doctor should advise her against travel for a week or two in her condition," Mr. Hardy agreed, "for her company shall be sorely missed! Sorely missed indeed! But there, my girl, don't you go takin' it into your head that you'll allow a passel of Overslate's relations to throw you into the hips! Why, you'll take the shine out of all of them. And don't you forget for a moment that you're to be the duchess! You're Augustus Hardy's daughter, first and last, and I daresay there's not a one of them that will look as fine as you will!"

Cordelia made no reply, but Betty, seated beside her mistress, nodded vehemently and took up the cause. "You listen to your pa, Miss Cordy! I've packed all of your best jewels and your fine Paris dresses, and you'll see that they cannot say that you are not in the first stare!"

Miss Hardy nodded, but inside, she still felt a little limp at the thought of being presented to her fiancé's relations. She wanted so much to please him, to make Overslate proud of her! And at the same time, her natural shyness made the approaching event an ordeal far worse than anything she had been put through in the metropolis. Her father and her maid meant well, of course, but she still fervently wished that she had the support of her friends Beau and Susannah. Castigating herself for being a selfish wretch when Susannah was confined to her bed with a cold—and in her condition!—Cordelia tried to smile brightly.

She would be with her beloved Harry again, and that was what she wanted, after all. This thought made her feel somewhat more sanguine. As the coach came to a lumbering halt before the portico of Overslate Castle, she peered anxiously outward, hoping for a glimpse of his face.

Neither Cordelia nor her father had perceived ought amiss when the duke had announced his departure for Overslate Castle shortly after he had made his proposal to Miss Hardy. In the brief visit he had paid to father and daughter at Claridge's, he had explained that pressing business forced him to separate from his fiancée before the last embers of the season had flickered and died. And he would not hear of spoiling her own plans by asking them to accompany him now, he had added quickly. Rather, he hoped that they would be his guests at a small family party to be held at the castle at the beginning of September.

Miss Hardy allowed herself to believe that he had gone ahead to make preparations for her visit, and Mr. Hardy, after assuring himself that the announcement of the forthcoming nuptials would be appearing in the journals for all to see, was willing enough to see his future son-in-law depart from the metropolis without setting up a wedding date. Having accomplished his mission, Hardy was content to receive a phalanx of persons representing his future son-in-law's interests, and spent a great deal of his time closeted with men from the City involved with the mysterious processes of settlement and dowry. Having satisfied himself that the bargain was irrevocable with the appearance of the announcements in the periodicals, he was prepared to be very generous indeed.

A Miss Hardy engaged to be married to the Duke of Overslate, it would seem, was of far more interest than a Miss Hardy of Baltimore with nothing to recommend her save a vulgarly new fortune and a vague connection to an obscure country baronetcy. Almost from the very day that the announcement had appeared in the *Morning Post,* tongues had wagged, and speculation upon the size and extent of Miss Hardy's fortune and antecedents across the Atlantic had run wild through the ton. It was variously said, and by those who ought to have known better, that her father had dowered her with her weight in gold, that she had been raised in the wilderness by wild Indians, and that Overslate had been bought out of the Fleet by the vast resources of Augustus Hardy. All but the very highest sticklers suddenly became quite curious to meet the future Duchess of Overslate. If they had been easily able to ignore her quiet presence in their midst before, even Miss Hardy's talent for self-effacement could not make her invisible now, and hostesses, piqued by curiosity and hungry, at this point in the season, for some new novelty to stimulate their dulled appetites, vied for her presence at their gatherings. In very short order, Cordelia was whirled into a series of out balls, balloon ascensions, water parties, masques, and fêtes, where, somewhat to her embarrassment, she was the object of careful scrutiny. If it had not been for the presence of her chaperons, the Southbies, whose ton was always impeccable, she might have been made the object of mockery for her American manners and the decidedly ostentatious manner in which her father considered it appropriate to garb his only offspring. It was fortunate that Susannah, whose taste was excellent, was there to curb the worst of Mr. Hardy's excesses on his daughter's behalf. There were those who remarked upon Harry's precipitate departure from London at such a crucial juncture, and the absence of the future bridegroom was much remarked upon in many quarters, but Cordelia, loyal in her love, defended him with the same excuses he had given her. If Beau and Susannah blithely credited Harry with a singular dislike of social events and a concern for his estates in the wake of a spate of bad weather in the West Country, Cordelia was more than willing to accept it as truth, and she did her best, despite her own shyness, to represent them both.

This new popularity left her little time for any speculation upon Harry's thoughts, and she was not enlightened by as much as a hastily scrawled note. But each day, a fresh nosegay of flowers was delivered to her by one of London's most tonnish florists, and in the absence of any note, she believed them to be proof of her fiancé's devotion. Susannah's blithe assurances that her cousin was the most wretched correspondent alive went a goodly distance in quelling any doubts that Cordelia might have entertained.

Her activities also precluded Gunther Shadwell's many attempts to seize a private moment with his employer's well-dowered daughter. Although Shadwell had not been made privy to his employer's thoughts upon his daughter's forthcoming marriage, he was, in the course of his duties, quite well aware of the financial arrangements being made for the match, and, if anything, the fact that Mr. Hardy was so willing to make a generous settlement only increased Shadwell's avarice. That Miss Hardy stood ready to marry another man was not something that so supreme a schemer as Mr. Shadwell would allow to deter him from his goals. A setback such as this made him even more determined, and he merely redoubled his habit of lingering at keyholes and investigating documents not addressed to his notice. Gunther Shadwell was nothing if not resolute, and bit by bit, he was carefully assembling a true picture of the circumstances concerning Miss Hardy's engagement.

"Man the fort, Shadwell!" Mr. Hardy adjured his man as the procession departed for the West Country.

"You may count upon me, sir!" Shadwell said with a bow, watching the carriages moving slowly out into the street, rubbing his palms together with a dry scraping sound, gleeful at this opportunity for an orgy of uninterrupted espionage.

True to his own dictum that everything must be first-rate, Mr. Hardy had taken extraordinary pains to assure himself that a day-and-a-half journey and a fortnight's visit would be conducted with all the pomp and ceremony of a royal procession. His twin goals were to assure himself that nothing apertaining to his own or his daughter's comfort would be neglected, and to be certain that the Hardys would hold their own against the Chrisfields in every matter of appearance and style. Since it was his deeply held conviction that the best way to travel was to provide oneself with goods for every possible contingency, no less than three coaches had been provided, giving the train the look of a Conestoga train heading for the deepest Louisiana Territory.

In the first carriage, a baggage wagon, all the portmanteaux, trunks, and bandboxes had been laden in, containing all the various costumes and ensembles that Mr. Hardy considered imperative for himself, his daughter, and their servants to appear to best advantage and consequence. Several wicker hampers containing every object that he considered indispensable for comfort against the rigors of country living had also been added to this load, for Mr. Hardy was a believer that rural settings were invariably uncomfortable, perhaps because of a childhood passed in a drafty manor house.

The second coach, a vast, swaying vehicle of grand and ancient design, heavily upholstered in purple velvet and deeply sprung, was to contain himself, Miss Hardy, and her maid in the utmost luxury of bearskin rugs and cushions. Into this interesting conveyance, Betty, ever mindful of her mistress's comfort, had piled her dressing case, her largest jewel box, a traveling chess set, and a bandbox containing her embroidery and smelling salts and a variety of feminine toiletries for any emergency on the road. Mr. Hardy had added a hamper containing a picnic lunch lest any of them perish of hunger before the first stage was reached, several ledger books that he intended to give a good going-over, and a collection of ancient American newspapers that he had that day received in the mails from across the Atlantic.

Cordelia, settling herself into a small space in the middle of all of this, laughed, suggesting perhaps that it might be fortunate that the Southbies had had to postpone their journey, since they would have been dreadfully squeezed to find space in such a pelter of goods.

Untroubled, Mr. Hardy replied that it had been his intention to provide them with a coach of their own, and that every attention would have been paid to Mrs. Southbie's care and comfort, to the extent of having her accompanied by her physician should the need arise.

That Beau had, against his spouse's protests, firmly

declined Mr. Hardy's generous offer served to puzzle Mr. Hardy considerably, but he was mollified by Beau's promise that they should come as soon as they were able to travel.

The last coach in this procession, with the defection of the Southbies, contained only Mr. Hardy's valet and two footmen that he considered necessary to his consequence, together with a last-minute addition of a large and irregularly shaped object, covered in several layers of wrapping, that Mr. Hardy referred to as a house gift for his future son-in-law. Cordelia was of half a mind to tease the contents out of her papa, but he took such pleasure in being mysterious about this object and seemed so certain that it would cause a great sensation that she finally lacked the heart to question him further about his surprise.

Lest the two females traveling with him be in the least concerned with their safety on this journey, the nabob made a great display of the large, heavily chased pistol that he carried in the pocket of his greatcoat. This, however, did not effect the desired result, as Betty, who had a strong aversion to guns, evinced signs of going into strong hysterics, and Cordelia pointed out that with four outriders, six postilions, and three coachmen, there was very little likelihood that even the most desperate of highwaymen would attack them on the road.

This led Mr. Hardy into some rather blood-curdling reminiscences on his days as a fur trader on the Natchez Trace, and in that spirit, the heavy conveyances lumbered through the traffic of London on the first stage of their journey.

With three heavily laden coaches and a score of attendant satellites, it was not to be wondered that Mr. Hardy's party did not reach their destination until the sun was setting over the western lawns, his daughter thought as she allowed one of her father's footmen to assist her in descent to the mounting block in the drive.

No sooner had her foot, neatly shod in halfboots, touched this stone than she beheld a sight that she would not soon forget.

From the path to the portico, the entire staff of Overslate Castle, attired in their very best, were assembled in a neat line, regarding the lady on the block with the blatant curiosity of those who are first beholding a new and untested force in their presence. This was not only the new duchess, but the lady whose fortunes would be the salvation of their jobs, and they were not unnaturally interested in this American of whom they had all heard so much since the duke's return to Overslate.

Cordelia, never at her best when twenty-five pairs of eyes were taking in every detail of her face and figure, estimating every penny she had paid for her clothing, felt herself flushing up to the roots of her hair, and her smile withering on her face. She felt very much as if she stood on the auction block at that moment, and the sight of her fiancé himself, very properly attired in evening clothes, ascending the steps and coming toward her did very little to allay her fears.

Harry, on his best dignity, was determined to be correct. If the Hardys wanted pomp and ceremony for their money, he was determined to give it to them, he decided, in the very best style of his grandfather's times.

"My dear Miss Hardy," Harry said in his best ducal manner, bowing low over Cordelia's hand as he helped her to descend to the ground. "Welcome to Overslate Castle—your future home!"

"Oh!" was all that Cordelia could think of to say, and she was reluctant to relinquish her grip on his hand. But Harry, determined that the Hardys should have a reception in the grand tradition, had already turned to the American nabob, inquiring if his future father-in-law had endured a safe journey.

Mr. Hardy was so far gone in a combination of alt at seeing his Cordy thus welcomed in a manner befitting a duchess and self-congratulations at his own foresight in making such a grand entourage for her that he too failed to note her discomfort.

Harry, with a raised eyebrow, gently but firmly disengaged Cordelia's hand from his own, tucking it beneath his arm as he turned and led her toward the gamut of assembled staff.

A tall and lofty individual of middle years with a

dignity that would have done credit to royalty detached himself from the head of the line and was introduced to Miss Hardy as Blackwood, his grace's steward.

Blackwood, in tones better suited to an Oxford don, presented Miss Hardy with a bouquet of flowers from "his grace's own houses," and earnestly hoped that, on behalf of the entire staff, he could welcome her to Overslate Castle as their future duchess with a great pleasure. With a great deal of roundaboutation and turns of phrase that made Cordelia's head spin, Blackwood continued on for some minutes about the tradition of service in the house of Chrisfield, and bade Miss Hardy know that the staff were here to serve their duchess with pride and the ceremony attendant on her rank.

Cordelia, rendered speechless, managed to stammer out an inaudible thanks before Harry led her down the line, introducing in turn his butler, his housekeeper, his head gardener, his coachman, and a succession of apple-cheeked maids, footmen, grooms, and undergardeners, all of them bobbing and curtsying to her with the liveliest interest.

Certainly no household belonging to Augustus Hardy was lacking in staff, but his servants were people Cordelia had known all of her life, people who had brought her up after her mother had died. These were strangers, regarding her as a threat, perhaps, or at the very least as an object of curiosity. She knew that she would be expected to recall all of their names, and already she had forgotten half of them. The very idea that she would be expected to give orders to such an individual as Blackwood made her want to faint.

At last, she stood upon the threshold of the house, but even here it would seem that there was to be no respite, for Harry was murmuring in her ear.

"I think that you might like to address the staff," he suggested. "It is expected."

Cordelia felt her heart sinking. She looked up at Harry imploringly, but his eyes were fixed on some distant and ducal point on the horizon.

"I thank you all very much!" she managed to say in a barely audible voice, and fell silent for several uncomfortable seconds before Mr. Hardy suggested that they might go inside.

"Just as you wish," Harry said, and threw open the door.

The Hardys were ushered into a vaulted hall of dreary gray stone that seemed to absorb whatever light filtered through the narrow windows. A fireplace so large that a tall man could stand and stretch within it was fitted into one corner, but the tiny fire that flickered in the grate gave no warmth to the high timbers or the damp stone floor.

"This is the oldest part of Overslate Castle," Harry informed his guests with a touch of pride. "It dates back to the Conquest." The sole ornaments of this chamber were a rusty suit of armor and an extremely uncomfortable-looking footman's chair of ancient pedigree that stood beside the high vaulted doorway. Cordelia, listening to their footsteps echoing across this empty space, felt as if she had entered the crypt, for the stone walls made it cold and damp, and there was a vague odor of mold.

"And this is the grand staircase," Harry continued, leading them into the next room, a more modern chamber from which a Jacobean double staircase led into the upper stories, and several doors led into other parts of the house. It had obviously, to Mr. Hardy's critical eye, seen better days, for the rugs and the upholstery on the Queen Anne sofa were dim. But, he noted, there was no mistaking the quality of the paneled wainscotting, and the Sh'ung vase that stood upon a table between the stairs was a priceless piece.

Harry touched his fiancée's hand briefly, and his eyes were filled with pride and love for his home. "This is Overslate!" he said, allowing himself to smile. "I imagine that you would like to go to your rooms and change for dinner now. Then perhaps you would join us in the library. Blackwood will show you to your rooms. When you are dressed, you might wish to ring for a footman. One of our best ghosts is a guest who was eternally lost, wandering the corridors of Overslate, looking for the dining room!" Harry shot off with a great deal of cheer, but the effect of his jest was lost upon Cordelia, who was inclined to look over her shoulder as if she expected to be confronted with a spectral presence.

Following the august thread of Blackwood up the long staircase, Mr. Hardy was given over to estimations of how much of his fortune it would take to bring Overslate Castle up to modern standards. A youth passed in the country houses of the quality had prepared him for this experience, but there was nothing in Cordelia's past to prevent her from a feeling of being overwhelmed by the high ceilings and heavy grandeur. Where Mr. Hardy saw dry rot in the wainscotting and chandeliers in need of replacement, Cordelia saw history, and wondered how she was to fare as mistress of such an establishment.

"Down-at-heel!" Mr. Hardy muttered beneath his breath, shaking his head. "Definitely down-at-heel!"

"His grace has given instructions for you to have the east wing," Blackwood informed them as they trudged down a long dark hall, followed by several footmen burdened down beneath the weight of their luggage. The steward halted them before a large, heavily carved oak door and turned the thick brass knob, looking toward Cordelia. "This is the Queen's Chamber," he informed her. "Her Majesty Elizabeth was pleased to stay here on her visit to Overslate in 1569."

"And to judge from the state of this room," Betty said, striding through the doorway, "it hasn't been aired since then! Here, you! Bring in those trunks, and mind that you're cautious with Miss Hardy's things!"

Blackwood, confronted with such heresy, cast the American maid a look of the purest horror, but Betty was not of a mood to tolerate him, and she directed herself to the placing of her mistress's many trunks, firmly shooing the footmen out the door and informing Blackwood that miss would require a jar of hot water sent up directly.

Cordelia, torn between laughter and frustration, shook her head. "Really, Betty, you should not set his back up!" she remonstrated, but the maid merely clucked her tongue.

"Indeed, miss! I won't have this passel of rogues

thinking that they can look down their noses at us, not while there's a breath in my body!" she scolded. "I have my orders from Mr. H., and look after your dignity I will, Miss Cordy! Now, you just strip out of that coat and warm yourself beside the fire while I tend to dressing you up like a duchess for dinner!"

Cordelia stood in the middle of the room, surveying the furnishings with awe. Ancient, faded tapestries covered the walls, depicting some particularly graphic scenes of a boar hunt, and not serving very well to block the drafts that seemed to emanate from the cold stone. A gargantuan bed, large enough to sleep an entire family, took up a great deal of the floor space, its four posts and head and foot boards covered with carvings of grotesques and gargoyles, the whole hung with what appeared to Cordelia to be hundreds of yards of crimson damask.

"I shouldn't wonder if Queen Elizabeth never slept a wink all night in that thing," she said, surveying it with dislike. "It is enough to give one nightmares!"

"And I'll wager that the sheets haven't been aired since her time, either," Betty said suspiciously. "And the fireplace smokes!" she added in horror as a burst of gray soot rolled down the chimney and spilled across the hearth rug. It was plain to see that Betty was utterly unimpressed with history. "What this place needs is a set of good Franklin stoves, such as we have back home in Baltimore. A stove and a bucket of coal!"

Cordelia suppressed a little chuckle, but shook her head. "Betty, we must not criticize!" she managed to say, a little doubt creeping into her voice. "After all, this is not our house!"

"But it will be yours, miss, and I can only hope that you don't suffocate in that bed!"

Neither female had any way of knowing that, in Harry's desire to give his fiancée's visit the fullest ceremony, they had been given the state apartments, a vast and pompous wing of the house that had not been used in a century.

Taking her cue from her surroundings, however, Betty began to unpack. "You'll be wanting to look your best tonight, miss, if you're to prove that you're a properly brought-up young lady and not some tawdry parvenu," the maid informed her mistress. "I think that you ought to wear your green gown, the one that you had made up in Paris, and the nice emerald set your papa bought you. You'll want to be at your grandest tonight to show them that you're a lady of consideration!"

Cordelia demurred, but her maid remained firm. "I won't have any of these high and mighty folks trying to say that you're an insignificant little dab of no particular consequence," she pronounced. "It reflects upon *me!*"

Cordelia, whose experience of visits to England country houses, or, indeed, any sort of a rural estate, was very limited, demurred by habit to her maid's opinions, vaguely regretting the absence of Mrs. Southbie even as she did so.

As a consequence, when she joined her father upon the landing an hour later, Mr. Hardy, whose experience of the great homes of England was thirty years in his past, also nodded with satisfaction. "Just as I would wish!" he said agreeably, casting an uncritical father's eye over Cordelia's toilette, and rubbing his waistcoat, a singular affair of embroidered daisies and forget-me-nots on a satin brocade of unforgettable scarlet. "No one would ever mistake you for anything but a duchess!" he exclaimed approvingly, patting his vast stomach and knotting his heavy brows.

Cordelia put a hand to her hair, piled high upon her head and encircled with an emerald band, beneath which Betty's carefully crimped curls fell about her face. "I feel so—so overdressed!" she admitted. "As if I were going to a state banquet!"

Mr. Hardy shook his head. "I want my daughter to look first-rate," he said meaningfully. "If we're to go up against the Chrisfields, we need to show them that the Hardys are of the best!"

Cordelia bowed to her father's opinions, but somehow could not help but feel that a dinner gown of *eau de nile* silk covered by an overskirt of Urling's lace, deeply hemmed in bands of blond satin bouffants, crimped with lozenges of lace, with cap sleeves slashed to reveal

90

eau de nile turban folds beneath more blond lace, with a deep corsage thickly ruched in alternating bands of gold satin and Urling's lace, was somehow not the gown she would have chosen for making her acquaintance with her future in-laws. Upon her feet, Betty had tied little slippers of gold and ivory stripe, and over one arm, she carried a heavily beaded reticule of bronze greekwork. Betty had delved into her mistress's jewel case and come up with her emerald set, an ensemble of deep-green stones set in tremblants of flowers and ivy, with the result that she appeared to be shimmering and tinkling with every step she took. In addition to the diadem, this set also included two bracelets, a necklet, and a pair of long earrings not particularly well suited to Cordelia's rather short neck, but again, Betty in her zeal to demonstrate her mistress's wealth had prevailed.

Mr. Hardy, however, was content, and offering his daughter his arm, they followed, in a small and stately procession, the guiding footman sent for them through a series of halls, galleries, and corridors toward the library.

By this circuitous route, the Hardys eventually reached a long gallery with several massive carved doors opening into the passageway. The footman unerringly chose one of these portals, and as his hands rested upon the brass knobs, the Hardys were able to hear the unmistakable sound of a female voice penetrating the thick wood. "—truly appalled, my dear Harry, to see the day when—"

The footman cleared his throat, throwing back the carved portals to expose a cavernous chamber that was, to Cordelia's mind, as far from a library as it would be possible to have. This was no cozy, book-lined study smelling of leather bindings and mahogany desks, but a stone-walled cave, hung with tapestries of ancient vintage and lined with shelves of carved wood from which it would appear that a great many volumes had long since disappeared.

Against the far wall, a group of persons were gathered about the huge stone fireplace, as much for warmth and light as for companionship, and in that little pool of life, all faces turned, all conversation ceased as the footman, in a toneless voice, announced, "Mr. Hardy and Miss Hardy!" before closing the doors and beating a hasty retreat to the warmth and light of the nether regions of the castle.

For several horrid seconds, Cordelia felt as if she were impaled upon the stares of these strangers, and she felt her shyness rising up to choke her, even as her eyes scanned the group desperately looking for Harry.

It would appear that the Hardys had interrupted a family scene, for a young female with the unmistakable olive cast of the Chrisfields, standing in the middle of the hearth rug before the fire, had placed a hand to her lips, and the duke himself seemed to have been in the act of rising from his chair to remonstrate with her.

There were so many of them, Cordelia thought, and yet the company could not have been above a half-dozen persons, turning their expressionless countenances from their own diversion, closing themselves off, even as they apprehended another. The gentlemen were rising to their feet, and she was startled to note how very tall members of the Chrisfield family tended to be, particularly in comparison to the rather diminutive stature of the Hardys.

Harry, caught unawares in the midst of whatever he had been saying to the young female with her hand to her mouth, had suddenly turned, his expression in that unguarded moment one of anger and annoyance at being interrupted. His eyes were as cold as ice, and his face was frozen into such a look of haughty contempt that Cordelia drew back a step, even as it passed from his face. It was not much, but it was enough to make her feel a tiny nagging doubt, as if she had perhaps misjudged the Duke of Overslate.

But Harry, all politeness and cordiality, was approaching them now, stepping outside of that firelit charmed circle to bid them welcome, impeccable and handsome in his evening dress, the perfect host whose eyebrow rose only a fraction of an inch when he drew Cordelia into the firelight and beheld her ensemble.

But if Harry considered himself no judge of feminine attire, it was clear that the Roman-nosed matron seated in the best wing chair beside the fire *did* consider herself an arbiter of matters of style, and that, in her cold gray eyes, the Hardys were *arrivistes.*

"Allow me to make you known to my aunt, Lady Armthea Southbie," Cordelia heard Harry saying, and her tremblants chimed at the way in which the formidable matron offered her two very stiff gloved fingers and a wintery stare.

It was clear, disastrously clear, to Cordelia that the good Betty had missed her mark, for Lady Armthea's dinner toilette in no way approached the elaboration of her own. The fifty-summered matron concealed her hair beneath a purple turban with a single ivory plume, and her lean form was clothed in a deceptively simple and, no doubt, hideously expensive dinner dress of murex silk, banded in dove-gray satin and the merest ruching of lace, with a ruff collar of starched muslin framing her angular head and shoulders. Her single ornament was a necklace of amethysts of ancient and singularly hideous mounting depending over her spare bosom, and about her shoulders she had draped a cashmere shawl against the prevalent drafts of Overslate Castle.

"How do you do," she said in tones as frosty as icy gusts, each word perfectly articulated, as if she were speaking to persons for whom English was a second language.

With one gloved hand, she raised a delicate lace handkerchief to her long nose, and Harry led the Hardys onward to face Lady Armthea's counterpart, an emaciated gentleman whose countenance and style showed unmistakable signs of dissipation, borne out by the order pinned to his chest proclaiming to the knowledgeable that he was a crony of the prince regent's.

"My uncle, Mr. Robert Southbie," Harry said, and leaning forward, in a slightly louder voice, the duke proclaimed in the older gentleman's ear, "Uncle Robert! Mr. Hardy and Miss Hardy!"

"I ain't deaf!" Uncle Robert said in the tones of one who is clearly impaired in just such a fashion. "And I ain't blind, either!" he added, surveying Cordelia and her father without enthusiasm. His handshake, Cordelia noted, was as limp as his spouse's, and she wondered that these two persons could have produced Beau Southbie.

"And this is my brother, Lord Victor Chrisfield," Harry continued on hastily.

A lank young man with his brother's eyes and a trace of adolescent spottiness lingering about his countenance shambled forward to mutter an inarticulate salute, his somewhat sullen expression suddenly and completely transformed when he beheld Mr. Hardy's waistcoat. "Oh, I say, sir," he exclaimed, all of his petulance abandoned, "that *is* something like!"

Cordelia suppressed a smile, for Lord Victor's choice in such matters was rival to her father's own in taste and style, being an eye-dazzling affair of alternating cherry-red and bottle-green stripes so lurid that even Miss Hardy, long inured to such sartorial displays, was forced to blink. But at least Mr. Hardy's waistcoat had won them one ally in this family, and she was inclined to think well of the Oxford undergraduate.

Harry was feeling his lips twitching also, although his reasons were completely different from Miss Hardy's. But his brows drew together when Lord Victor blurted out next, "They've just been raking me down for my vulgar taste in waistcoats, you know! But they're all the crack at Magdalen, and so I'll tell the world!"

Before Mr. Hardy could digest this piece of information, the duke had swiftly shuttled his guests on to the last member of his family, the young lady who had evidently been the cause of the altercation the Hardys' appearance had interrupted.

She had removed her hand from her lips, but two bright spots of color burned in her cheeks, and her eyes were flashing as she turned to greet the Hardys.

"My sister," Harry said dryly, "Lady Dorothea Chrisfield."

Cordelia noted that the girl had avoided the more unfortunate characteristics of adolescence that seemed to plague her twin, and was well upon her way to achieving the status of beauty, being much enhanced by a certain liveliness of spirit that shone in her face as she took Cordelia's hands into her own, and from her superior height, gazed down upon the smaller female with a tremulous smile. "*I* am very glad to meet you, and welcome to Overslate Castle!" Lady Dorothea announced in a slightly shaken voice, with a defiant look at her family. "And *I* like your gown!"

CHAPTER SEVEN

In the yawning chasm of silence which followed this remark, however well intentioned it might have been, Harry's tones were so loud as to enable even Mr. Southbie to hear them without the aid of his ear trumpet.

"Thea!" he exclaimed.

His sister gave him a sideways glance. "Well, I do!" she said. "I wish I had such gowns, instead of these rags that Aunt thinks it proper for me to wear!" With a distasteful gesture, Thea indicated her simple sprig muslin gown. "Now that Harry is marrying an—"

"That will be quite enough!" Harry told his sister in a dangerous tone of voice, and Thea looked rather startled.

"Did I say something wrong?" she asked naively.

But Cordelia, who had felt a delicate flush stealing up from her bodice, wished that a yawning pit would open up beneath her feet and swallow her into it. In her ears, as loud as churchbells, she heard the chiming of all of her emerald tremblants at once. Looking at Harry for comfort, she saw only his anger, and with a sinking feeling, realized that she had failed her first test as a duchess-to-be.

But Mr. Hardy seemed to have other thoughts. Secure with his whiphand over the same persons who had dismissed him as a penniless younger son some thirty years ago, he, at least, would now derive some amusement from his revenge. No barbs directed toward his displays of wealth could penetrate his thickened skin, and his laugh boomed out over the company.

"Now, Lady Thea, you are a sly puss and no mistaking it!" he chuckled approvingly. "A female without roundaboutation is a female to be admired, and I'll wager a good sum that you've already left a trail of broken hearts in your merry path!"

This speech was quite novel in Lady Dorothea Chrisfield's experience, as was such a person as Mr. Hardy himself, and she immediately fell beneath his spell, enthralled by her first conquest.

If Mr. Hardy's remarks encouraged Lady Thea's high spirits and unrestrained tongue, they could not be said to have the same effect upon the rest of the company, for Lady Armthea had pinned her basilisk stare upon them both, exuding indignation and *lèse majesté* from every pore, while Harry stood in the center of the room, an astounded frown upon his countenance, momentarily stunned into speechlessness.

"What? What?" Mr. Southbie asked querulously, and Lord Victor shook his head over the absurdly high points of his collar.

"You," Lady Armthea said imperiously, waving a hand at Cordelia, "will please come and sit beside me." Her plume nodded. "Harry! Get Miss Hardy a chair!"

Cordelia looked toward her fiancé for reassurance, and found none there, as Harry wordlessly obeyed his aunt's commands.

With every emerald glittering in the firelight, Cordelia obediently settled herself beside Lady Armthea, trembling beneath that same basilisk gaze, for the several seconds it took that matron to assess her toilette in close proximity.

"It," the *grande dame* finally announced, "is totally unprecedented to have an American in the family."

Since this was stated in the same tones that might have been used to note the absence of transported criminals and hopeless madmen in the family tree, Cordelia could think of no reply, and another awkward silence fell about the company by the fire, in high contrast to the group on the sofa, where the novel Georgian charm of Mr. Hardy was not lost upon Lady Thea, and had, indeed, managed to draw Lord Victor, perhaps attracted by such a notable waistcoat, into the orbit of the merchant prince.

Harry, for whom a lifetime spent with Aunt Southbie had left him immune to the terror she could provoke in less confident individuals, felt a vague sense of annoyance with his fiancée's lack of conversation. Aunt was, after all, a part of the entire package, and if Miss Hardy aspired to become a duchess, it behooved her to attempt to get along with the lady whom she would replace as mistress of Overslate Castle. It did not occur to him that his betrothed might require rescuing from such a formidable dame as his aunt.

"Americans? Americans at Overslate?" Uncle Robert said at that moment, having laboriously strained for the drift of his spouse's conversation. "Must be one of Beau's ideas! Prinny says—"

What the regent might have had to say about Americans was never to be known, for at that moment, the double doors opened, and several persons entered the room, greeting Lady Armthea in such styles as defined their kinship within the family. Since this group was shortly followed by another and then another, the room was soon very full indeed of Chrisfields and relations in varying degrees of connection to that noble house.

It was clear that they had been summoned from their various abodes in the country with the sole purpose of ceremoniously greeting the future duchess at the request of the head of the family. And while they may have varied widely over the spectrum of humanity in terms of style, physiognomy, and fortune, as Cordelia was presented to each one, and struggled in vain to remember their names and their degrees of kinship to Harry, one thing at least was very clear to her—they belonged to a closed, self-contained world into which she would be admitted only on tolerance. It was not that their smiling faces were rude or mocking as they took her hand and surveyed her dress; oh, no, they were far too polite for *that*, she sensed with an increasing sense of her own inadequacy, her own alienation from their world. It was something intangible in their manners, some stiffness in those smiles that never quite reached their eyes, that seemed to repulse her away from them even as they murmured their congratulations and their welcomes.

And while many of the women were gowned in the first style of fashion, none were so elaborate as she.

Parvenu, she seemed to read from their looks. *American nobody.*

As the butler passed the sherry, and the company, already diversified by outlook and occupation, claiming only their kinship and their class for a bond, began to circulate through the room, she was glad enough to withdraw to a chair well removed from the center of activity, all but ignored, even by her fiancé, who barely seemed to note her disappearance from the center of the stage.

Indeed, so humiliated did Cordelia feel by her own sartorial display, her own gaucheness, that she was almost grateful to assume her accustomed position of wallflower, feeling quite crushed by this gathering of lofty strangers.

It was over a quarter-hour before Harry recalled his future bride and scanned the room in search of her. Seeing her sitting alone, her sherry untouched in the glass in her hand, her brown eyes rather longingly following every move that he made, he frowned. What, he wondered, did women want? Here he had gone to a great deal of trouble to assemble this pack of ravenous, perfectly dreadful relations, solely to please her sense of consequence, and she was not even attempting to ingratiate herself with them. Not that he had ever made the slightest push to do more than acknowledge any of this myriad kin when reminded of their existence, but under the impression that Cordelia would wish to assert her kinship with some of the most fashionable and powerful members of the ton, he would have expected her to be pushing herself to their notice.

He ran a finger around his collar, supposing that it behooved him to go over and at least attempt to draw her into the conversation. Damn, what did women want?

Oblivious to her trepidation, he made himself smile as he walked across the room, seating himself beside her. He did not note the way in which her countenance illuminated in his presence, but settled himself comfortably beside her, crossing one leg over the other and surveying the room.

"That's the family—at least most of 'em, anyway!" he said blithely, and was tempted to add that Cousin Serena, the one in red, lived in a house in Bath with forty-two cats, or that Lord Trevor, the cousin with the receding chin and the highly dandified air, had been for many years on the most intimate terms with a series of very handsome and very stupid young footmen in his household, or that his second cousin Caroline had once been a favorite of a royal duke, with the result that she was now saddled with a pack of the most frog-faced unmarriageable daughters ever to appear at Almack's. In short, he viewed his kin as either very dull persons or loose screws worthy of amusement, but somehow he did not think that this jaded opinion would impress Miss Hardy with his own desirability as a mate, so instead, he remarked, "Thrown the house open to them for the week. Good chance for you to get to know us all."

"They all seem very interesting," Cordelia remarked, a little dully. "So many of them! But if they are your relations, I shall do my best to—that is, I am certain that I shall like them all!"

Harry threw her a glance, and saw no humor in her expression. "There are a lot of them," he admitted. And they'll eat me out of house and home, and probably tear up the south lawn with croquet, he thought. But as long as this is the grand ceremonious sort of thing that you want, you shall have it. And welcome, he appended to himself. Aloud he said, "And they are to be your family also, you know. You'll have to recall their birthdays and christenings and weddings and funerals and whatnot. Aunt Southbie will instruct you in what you should send or write. If you have any questions, you must ask her! She's far more consequent than I about such affairs." He nodded agreeably. "Since m'mother died, she's been hostess and *doyenne* of Overslate, you see. Left everything about the servants and so forth to her. But now that you're here, Miss Hardy, she'll be turning over her keys to you. Show you how to go on and so forth."

Cordelia, watching Aunt Southbie's finely chiseled profile as she raised her head to greet a dowager in gray silk, felt a shiver of doubt run through her spine.

"I wouldn't dream of disturbing Lady Armthea—been here so long, knows how things should be—" Cordelia managed to stammer out.

"Nonsense! You're the duchess now, or you very soon will be! Doubtless Aunt and Uncle Southbie will retire to the dower house, and go to Brighton for the season—they're great friends of the prince regent's. At least," he added thoughtfully, with a little laugh, "Uncle Robert is! M'aunt's too high a stickler to approve of our beloved Prinny's ways! Whatever, you need only look to her for advice and she will be glad to help you."

This Cordelia was inclined to doubt, but said nothing. Instead, she turned to Harry and, summoning her courage, slipped one hand into his own.

"I shall try to do my best to make you happy," she said. "We have had so little time together—"

He patted her hand, returning it to her lap. "Not here, Miss Hardy! Won't do, even for an engaged couple, to be mooning about in a corner, you know! Now, come and meet my third cousin once removed, Lady Easton! Beau and I were both quite moonstruck over her when we were lads."

By her mere entrance into the library, a strikingly beautiful woman seemed to electrify what had previously been a rather dull gathering. Her blond beauty was of the most delicate porcelain tones, and her smile, bestowed upon everyone, radiated an enchantment that hinted at sunlight bursting suddenly upon a cloudy afternoon. She moved with a leonine grace, her delicately simple and elegant gown of champagne silk moving with the curves of her body to expose a glimpse of a lithe, sensual figure without the least whisper of vulgarity that might have attended a lesser female attempting the effect. From all corners of the room, she was being converged upon by her male relations, graciously accepting the compliments paid to her by a roué uncle, tactfully turning aside the stammered admiration of an awkward young cousin as she made her way toward Aunt Southbie, still seated in her throne beside the fire.

Lady Armthea's dour face actually illuminated into a smile at the appearance of this damsel, and she lifted one thin cheek to receive a kiss from those rosy lips.

"Late as always!" this lady said, holding up a little nosegay of flowers. "But someone placed these in my room, and I just had to choose a gown to compliment my admirer!"

Aunt Southbie clucked indulgently. "Charlotte, you were always a shocking flirt, my dear!"

"I know, and isn't it dreadful? But I am just out of black gloves for Easton, you know, so it behooves me to look my best!" She looked about the room, nodding and smiling as she caught each eye. "And where, pray tell, is Harry? I am dying to meet the female who has finally managed to snag my dearest Overslate!"

"Here I am, Charlotte! I am glad that you could come!" Harry said, leaving Cordelia in his wake as he greeted his cousin with open admiration. "You're looking remarkably well, you know!"

Lady Easton pealed as she gave Harry a peck on the cheek, holding him at arm's length to survey his person with her green eyes. "I swear, you haven't changed a bit since you came back from Spain, Overslate! In fact, you are even more handsome than ever! Aren't I dreadful? It is quite improper of me to come out of black a full month early, but when I had your letter saying that you were getting married, I just had to come and see the female you'd snagged for your own!

"Oh, yes," Harry said, almost as if it were an afterthought, stepping aside to reveal Cordelia to Lady Easton's interested gaze. "Uh, Miss Hardy, may I present Lady Easton, m'cousin?"

Cordelia was not slow to see the flickering look of disbelief and assessment that passed across the other woman's face before she extended one gloved hand. "Well, I am just charmed to meet you!" Lady Easton said, and her smile did not reach her eyes, but rather seemed to indent the sides of her pretty mouth with the most infinitesimal lines of contempt. "I've heard so much about you! With my late husband passed, I've been rusticated in mourning for just ages and ages, but my friends in London managed to keep me up with the news, and you were certainly on everyone's lips, Miss Hardy!"

Someone, Cordelia was not quite certain who, snickered, but Lady Easton continued to smile, exuding sincerity. "You know, I *never* thought Harry would marry," she continued with a little tinkling laugh. "When we were just knee-high, he always *swore* that his heart would belong to me forever and ever. Aren't men just too odious for words? And you're an American, I understand. That must be very interesting. We do things so much differently over here. Overslate, I am just dying for a tiny glass of sherry." She looped her arm into Harry's, gazing up at him charmingly.

"Excuse me," Harry murmured to Cordelia, and allowed himself to be led away by Lady Easton, leaving Miss Hardy alone in the middle of the floor.

"—so amusing!" her voice drifted back.

Without allies, Cordelia drifted back to her chair in the corner, watching numbly as Lady Easton flitted from person to person in the room with Harry in her wake.

"I have always said that dear Charlotte would have made such an excellent duchess," Mr. Southbie said, and in spite of his wife's warning look, his words drifted toward Cordelia, who felt as if she had been slapped. "Particularly now that Easton's stuck his spoon in the wall and left her everything! Always thought she and Harry would make a match of it if things had worked out for the best!"

To add to Cordelia's misery, the steward appeared

at that moment to announce that dinner was served, and she watched as every female in the room save herself was given the escort of a gentleman to dinner. The lively Thea had managed to ensnare Mr. Hardy, and Cordelia's heart twisted inside her breast to watch Harry gallantly giving his arm to Lady Easton. If he loved her as he said he did, she thought, confused, why did he not look at her in just such a way?

"Miss Hardy?"

Cordelia looked up to see Lord Victor standing over her, offering his arm with an awkward smile. Gratefully she rose and placed her hand in the crook of his elbow, allowing her to join him in the procession of couples meandering through the long corridors toward the dining room.

"I say," he murmured awkwardly, "I think it will be grand to have you in the family. Your pater is something like, you know! He's not one to ring a peal over your head about some prank or another one's pulled at university! *He* regards them as a very good joke, and will tell you about the time that he was rusticated for putting a goat in the bagwig's rooms!"

Cordelia, rightly suspecting that her father was being compared to Overslate's guardianship, wisely said nothing, but felt glad that she had found at least one ally in this nest of strangers.

The dining hall was part of the most ancient structure of the castle, and had been largely unaltered since the days when the Chrisfields presided over a vast feudal fortress. Its high vaulted ceilings were supported by buttresses of original Gothic design, and the gray stone walls were partially, and rather ineffectually, protected from drafts by a series of ancient and rather depressingly done tapestries depicting some forgotten battle in which the Chrisfields had played a major part. At one end of this enormous chamber yet another gargantuan hearth burned a log, but there was not sufficient heat to prevent the damp and chill of centuries from permeating every corner of the room. Banners of the Chrisfield arms were suspended above this hearth, and some thoughtful and provident ancestor had caused the ancient flambeaux to be replaced with modern crystal chandeliers, providing at least a little warmth and light for the diners at the long table, now set with the best service. To be sure, some of the plates were a little chipped, and the gilt was sadly worn through, but beneath the light of a thousand candles, it gave Cordelia a sense of what ducal splendor must be like.

Into this imposing hall trooped all of the Chrisfield relations, and though there might have been twenty of them seated about the long table, there would easily have been room for twenty more with only the slightest cramping of elbows.

The duke took his place at the head of this long board, and Aunt Southbie had hers at the foot. The seating arrangement must have been of her design, for Cordelia found herself situated between the disdainful Uncle Southbie and a terrifyingly fashionable dandy with a decidedly feminine air whom she deduced, from the score of relations she had been presented to that evening, was the duke's cousin Viscount Trevor.

It was not fated to be a pleasant dinner in any respect. The first course, arriving from a kitchen hall nearly an eighth of a mile from the table, was spooned into the plates as a lukewarm turtle soup, and Uncle Southbie made no time wasted in sourly and rather loudly complaining that the food at Prinny's table in Brighton was far superior to that of his own home.

Cordelia, fighting down her shyness, attempted valiantly to delve further into the interests and occupations of a crony of the Prince of Wales, but found Uncle Southbie's deafness increased with each timid conversational sally she made, until she was left with the uncomfortable feeling that had she been younger and more attractive, some of that dissipated hauteur might have thawed into a rather unbecoming flirtation. Since Uncle Southbie clearly had sacrificed the pleasures of an extended visit with his sovereign to do his duty by a fiancée of whom it was evident to Cordelia he did not approve, she was forced to dip her spoon into her soup and bring the empty bowl to her lips while she listened to a series of non sequiturs contrasting the company of Prinny and his friends to the deadly boredom of a family party.

It was with a feeling of considerable relief that she saw the green and viscous soup, now quite cold, removed from her place and replaced by the usual fish course, of turbot and salmon aspic, feeling that even the tonnish chill of Lord Trevor was preferable to the crotchets of Uncle Southbie.

At the head of the table, a merry peal of laughter rang out, and Cordelia glanced up to see Lady Easton, quite glowing with smiles, playfully slapping at Harry's hand with her fan. Perhaps a little of what she was feeling appeared upon her face, for Trevor's opening gambit was uttered in a decidedly dry voice.

"Dear Charlotte always was a charmer," he remarked, turning in his seat, since the high points of his collar prevented him from turning his head toward his partner. "So used to being the focal point of every gathering."

Although Cordelia was prevented from seeing his expression by the height of his shirt points and the elaboration of his cravat, she had a distinct feeling that he was smiling, and raised her chin slightly so that her own commonsensical gaze met his.

"Yes, I daresay, it is ever so with ladies who are judged upon their beauty," she admitted a little gruffly.

Lord Trevor threw his head back slightly and gave a laugh. "Here now, Miss Hardy! You shall ruin my cravat entirely if you make me laugh, and that would never do. My man spent a full hour arranging it for me, and would be quite cast into the sulks if I were to ruin his handiwork." He managed to shake his head slightly from side to side, making a delicate gesture with one fine-boned hand, upon which several rings glittered in the light.

Cordelia, whose experience of such gentlemen as Lord Trevor was very definitely limited, managed not to stare, but the viscount, without even the semblance of feigning interest in his fish course, managed to assess her with a shrewd eye. "Fascinating tremblant work," he murmured, with another airy gesture toward her jewels. "Parisian, I think, and probably *ancien regime?* Ah, it is quite off-putting to think of the poor lady for whom that set was created, whose delicate neck was ornamented by so fine a piece, falling beneath the blade." He shook his head sadly and sighed. "It quite makes me lose my appetite to contemplate it, you know. I dislike bloodshed. So—unappealing. But that lady's misfortune is evidently your gain, Miss Hardy, and for that, we must be happy, for I have never seen a better example of tremblant work."

"I know nothing about jewels, I fear," Cordelia said frankly. "My father purchased these for me as a gift in Paris."

"I thought it might have been Mr. Hardy's choice," Trevor drawled, lifting his wineglass to his lips with an extended finger.

"Papa likes jewels, you see, and he likes to see women in them."

"Mmmm," Trevor agreed, casting a look toward Mr. Hardy, who seemed happily involved in a conversation with a rather astonished dowager of uncertain years and wearing a great deal of rouge. "And doubtless he will be in alt to see you in the jeweled crown of a duchess. Not quite as pretty, really, as those emeralds, but a prize beyond their price."

Cordelia poked at her fish with a fork. It was not particularly well prepared, she thought, and was astonished again by the fact that the English seemed so indifferent to the value of well-done meals. "You talk over my head, my lord," she said at last.

"Do I?" Trevor drawled, studying her closely. "I think not. Although our paths have not crossed in London— Almack's is not precisely my stomping ground, you understand!—let us say that your reputation preceded you. But you are an intimate of dear Beau and Susannah, are you not? It is a pity that they are not here to protect you from the buffets of this family. One must never doubt Beau and Susannah's ton, of course, but they are so apt to become depressingly freethinking and modern in their choice of associations. Doubtless it comes from Beau's involvement in politics. Whig politics at that; quite, quite heretical, I fear—in the family. When I heard that Harry was actually doing this thing, of course, I knew that I had to drop all of my engagements and simply rush off to the country—such a dismal place!—to watch the fun!"

Cordelia regarded him flatly. "I suppose it would be amusing to you," she said with more complacency than she was feeling.

"My dear young woman, *everything* amuses me," the viscount returned, completely unruffled. "If I had not long ago learned to develop the skin of an elephant and the defenses of a hedgehog, the chances are excellent that I would be quite, quite beyond the pale." For an instant, his eyes became deadly serious as they rested upon Cordelia's. "For, you see, my dear Miss Hardy, I too know what it feels to be on sufferance, the knowledge of what is said behind my back, the little smiles, the little cuts." He waved a hand about the board. "Particularly in the company of my dear relations. Were I not a perfectly acceptable gentleman in almost every respect—including, of course, a rather tidy fortune that places me in a most independent position from the censure of these griffons—I should have long ago departed for a life on the Continent, another black sheep gone and forgotten. *Comprendez?*"

"Yes," Cordelia admitted slowly.

The viscount's eyes twinkled. "I thought that you might. It is always easy to recognize a fellow sufferer, cut from the pack. But, my dear, if I may venture to drop a word into your ear, it takes far more than mere lucre to allow one to be admitted into the ranks. It takes, let us say, a certain originality, a certain courage, a certain *je ne sais quoi*. Panache? Yes! Panache! The very word! Exquisite of me, I must remember that! A certain way of being—"

Miss Hardy sighed. "But I am not at all good at that sort of thing, as you can see. Not like Lady Easton, or Lady Armthea. I am simply me, and despite all of Papa's efforts, you cannot turn a silk purse from a sow's ear. That is why I was so surprised when Overslate proposed to me—that he should feel as I do—"

Cordelia, with a feeling of indiscretion, dropped her eyes, biting her lip. Truly, this man was confusing to her, first seeming so sympathetic, and then so mocking. She raised her chin slightly. "I may not have been born to this world, but I am determined that our feelings for one another shall not be crushed out by anything that his family might feel! I am determined to make Harry a good duchess, if that is what he wishes me to become!"

"And what of yourself? Doing it too brown, Miss Hardy! Becoming Duchess of Overslate is, after all, no easily accomplished task. Surely you cannot deny a, shall we say, certain enjoyment in picturing yourself in that role?"

Her eyes very wide, Cordelia looked up at the viscount. "I wish to be a good wife to Harry," she said firmly. "And therefore, it seems that I shall have to become a good duchess. Or, at least, a duchess," she added a little doubtfully. "At any rate, it pleases Papa."

A chortle issued from the depths of Lord Trevor's neckcloth. "I beg of you, Miss Hardy, I must not laugh! Truly, I must not! Disarrange my neckcloth and that would never do! It must be the fashion among couples this season to speak of love! Romantics, perhaps! Influence of Byron and Shelley! Come now, Miss Hardy! We are to be kin! You need have no delicacy of feeling with me, I assure you. Been an embarrassment to see the head of the family wracked up so badly! Glad to see an arrangement that will bail him out of the suds, whatever I might think of Harry as a person." He leaned toward her. "Besides, I shall be glad of some fresh blood in the family. Come now, Miss Hardy, from the moment I saw you, I credited you with a great deal of common sense."

"And very little sense of panache, also," Cordelia said dryly. "But I should prefer that virtue, if it makes Harry comfortable, to any of the thousand subtle little cynicisms that pass for tonnish manners!" She shifted her fish about on her plate. "And I intend to make Harry comfortable as best I can. Perhaps I am not so commonsensical as you believe, for I am foolish enough to think that love between two persons may overcome a great many other obstacles."

"By God, I do believe that you are in love with Overslate!" the viscount said at last, surprise in his voice.

At that moment, the fish was replaced by the beef course, accompanied by several different types of vegetables, all of them depressingly cold when served, and accompanied by the standard lobster, mint, and *jus* boats, which did little to brighten the fact that everything was overcooked and soggy.

For such a lean man, Uncle Southbie ate with gusto, but Cordelia noted that like many others at the table, he seemed to apply himself with far more enthusiasm to the selection of heavy wines that accompanied each course, imbibing with a prodigality that she found truly astonishing.

Several glasses of hock, however, served to thaw him out to the point where he was able, in an entirely one-sided conversation, to lecture her, in a loud voice, upon the various misfortunes which had attended his wife's family for several generations, and this series of setbacks, mostly financial, and all of them somehow blamed upon the politics of the Liberal Party, did little to brighten her spirits or leave her with the impression that the Chrisfields had in any way distinguished themselves save at the gaming tables and in their ability to survive as one of the more titled families to be found among the Upper Ten Thousand. That no Chrisfield had made any outstanding contribution to the arts and sciences, to the governing of the country, to the fighting of its wars, or to the maintaining of its peace seemed not to bother Uncle Southbie in the least. Rather, it appeared to Cordelia, he seemed to feel that the very lack of any such distinguishing mark upon the pages of history was a most commendable virtue. To be a Chrisfield, he seemed to imply, was more than enough compensation for any lack of achievement. She was left, when the beef course drew to a close, with the feeling that Uncle Southbie regarded her as marrying into the ranks of Olympus. And very much, as Lord Trevor had remarked, on sufferance.

If things were decidedly dull at her end of the table, she was able to detect at Harry's end of the board a liveliness and gaiety that seemed to emanate from the general leadership of Lady Easton, who, Cordelia noted, seemed as full of some sort of esoteric wit as she was of obvious beauty. She spoke in a cant that Cordelia could only half comprehend, of persons and places of which Cordelia had no knowledge, in an attitude of self-assurance that was totally alien to Cordelia's nature. And it could not help but hurt her a little that Harry seemed completely beneath the spell of his beautiful cousin. He had not once returned her own glances toward his place at the table, seeming barely able to remove his eyes from Charlotte.

As the fowl course, braised duck in oyster sauce, was set before her, Cordelia heard Aunt Southbie's voice in the lull, speaking very clearly indeed.

"Of course, everyone has always said what an excellent duchess dear Charlotte would have made...."

Involuntarily, Cordelia's eyes met Lady Armthea's across the room, and the matron returned her gaze with that famous basilisk stare, her jaw working over her food as if she were a complacent dragon.

Cordelia's hand clutched very tightly at the napkin in her lap, and she turned her gaze again toward Lady Easton's place, just in time to catch the intimate way in which the beautiful widow had laid her hand across Harry's arm, leaning ever so delicately toward him, almost whispering something into his ear with smiling lips as her eyes met Cordelia's with a look of contempt. Lady Easton's smile was not contagious, for as she spoke, Harry was looking at Cordelia also, and a thin, deep line appeared between his brows, as if he were reassessing her in the light of some not particularly pleasant truth brought to his attention by his cousin.

Cordelia felt her heart pounding heavily in her breast, and in that moment, she wanted nothing more than to pick up her skirts and run, to plead a headache, anything that would remove her from the room. It was true, she realized unhappily. Lady Easton, so beautiful, so assured, so at ease in this strange world, would have made the perfect duchess of Overslate. Cordelia made as if to rise from her chair, but felt the gentle pressure of Trevor's delicate fingers upon her arm.

"Sit down," he said without looking at her. "And for God's sake, smile at me! I wondered how long it would take you to catch the lay of the land, Miss Hardy."

Cordelia did as she was told, a ghastly parting of the lips that was more grimace than smile.

The viscount's fingers continued to dig into her arm, however, and she managed to still the beating of her heart with a sip of her wine.

"Do you know," Trevor said thoughtfully, "I think *I* would have made a better duchess than either one of you. And certainly I would manage this household—if not my tongue!—with far more panache than dear Aunt Southbie, may she roast in hell in her own juices," he added pleasantly, raising his glass to his aunt.

"I am not precisely certain that I understand," Cordelia managed to stammer out.

The viscount *tsked*. "I told you that I had arrived in this godforsaken place solely for the entertainment. Surely Beau and Susannah must have told you all about dear Charlotte and Harry? Quite an affecting tale, I assure you!" He raised his napkin delicately to his lips. "Smile, Miss Hardy! The family is watching! And I assure you, grace beneath pressure is a prime asset for any duchess."

Cordelia nodded, although she was far from feeling gay.

"Well!" Trevor continued, shaking his head. "It is really simply too odious of Beau and Susannah to neglect to mention dear Cousin Charlotte. But I suppose, in their own well-meaning way, they pictured her safely stowed away in the wilds of the north still wearing the weeds, if not the willow, for poor Easton! In their anxiety to see Overslate suitably fixed with the appropriate female, no doubt it was necessary to gloss over dear Charlotte. Naughty of them, I fear, but nonetheless practical. Indeed, I doubt if Overslate himself would have given her much thought if it had not been for the machinations of Aunt Southbie. Yes, I am certain that I see her fine Italian hand in all of this!" Lord Trevor shook his head regretfully. "It is a great deal too bad that the Chrisfield side of the family has always been sadly lacking in Machiavellian instincts. So *very* unsubtle! So exactly what one would expect from the old dragon, particularly since Beau would insist upon marrying Susannah, who may have a trade connection in her own background, you know!"

"No, I did not know," Cordelia said, and fired by wine

courage, added, "but I am certain that you will tell me all!"

"My pleasure, my dear Miss Hardy. It would seem that before Overslate went off to the wars, he and dear cousin Charlotte conceived a mild *tendre*. Oh, I am certain that it was nothing but a young man's fancy toward the reigning belle in the face of an unknown future and all of that sentimental pish-pash." He waved a hand in a delicate gesture of dismissal. "But of course, Aunt Southbie, being such a frightful high stickler, simply adores Charlotte. Charlotte, my dear, is a lady from head to toe—and inside, I would venture to suggest that the only heart that could possibly be blacker or more ambitious than that which pounds in her ample bosom is my own—a little-known fact, but a true one, you see! Cousin Charlotte's parents, being Chrisfields, were, of course, as poor as churchmice, and it was necessary that their very lovely daughter make an advantageous match to save the family fortunes. Lord Easton was very rich and very old. I fear that it was not the happiest match, for he was also only a mere earl, and I don't doubt that Charlotte played him fast and loose from the moment the ring was on her finger. Oh, very discreetly, of course—Charlotte is a born hypocrite— but I do not doubt, if I may sully your virgin ears with such thoughts, that the late and most unlamented Lord Easton died with a smile on his face."

Cordelia nodded without flinching as the viscount's eyes met her own. "Perhaps, indeed, I am certain that her fortune could not be a drop in the ocean compared to your own—those emeralds, my dear, are exquisite and quite, quite worth the moon and stars, however inappropriate they may be to a simple family dinner in the country. But I digress! Easton did leave his bereaved widow a very warm woman. And a woman anxious to rise again in her station in life, to a station that would fulfill all of her social ambitions. As Countess of Easton, she was, shall we say, adequate, but as Duchess of Overslate—well! You do understand! Very good! In short, my dear Miss Hardy, I am absolutely convinced that our dear Charlotte, in general always so observant of all the outward proprieties of custom by

113

which such dragons as Aunt Southbie set such store, has managed to put away her black gloves to make her appearance at this festive little gathering solely at the instigation of dear, dear Lady Armthea Southbie. You see, Charlotte is one of us, and quite the apple of Aunt's wretched fishy eye. While you, Miss Hardy, however interesting, however well endowed, are, well, an *American*."

"I see," Cordelia said in a tiny little voice. "She is fascinating," she had to add in all honesty. "And she would make such a duchess...."

"But my dear Miss Hardy, would she make Overslate a good wife?"

Cordelia, feeling quite cast down, could not quite read the expression in her dinner partner's eyes. Perhaps he was mocking her, like all the rest.

CHAPTER EIGHT

Cordelia's ordeal did not end after the last drops of *sorbet* had been spooned, nor the final bite of the *gateaux au chocolat* consumed, for Lady Armthea gave the signal for the withdrawal of the ladies, leaving the gentlemen to their politics and port over the board.

Dutifully trailing the rest of the ladies, their dresses rustling, she followed her hostess through yet another series of winding passageways toward yet another vast and vaulted chamber Aunt Southbie was pleased to term the Gold Salon.

Gold it might have been at one time, Cordelia thought, but everywhere there was evidence of a sad state of decay and neglect. The curtains were sadly faded from their original brocaded luster to a dull mustard color, and the upholstery on the furniture was badly frayed. The Italianate landscapes on the walls stood in need of the restorer's cleaning, and to Cordelia, who had prided herself on her keeping of her father's houses since the day she had become their chatelaine, poverty was no excuse for the dust in the corners nor the unraveling of a tassel on a gilt footstool.

Doubtless, Miss Hardy thought, seating herself a little distance from the tea table and the fire, where she could watch as Aunt Southbie poured from a disgracefully tarnished teapot, that matron was far too given over to her own consequence as the daughter of a duke to give affairs of housekeeping any note, but it was not to her credit that Miss Hardy could have written her name in the dust on a Queen Anne table.

Her contemplation of the deplorable standards of Aunt Southbie's housekeeping completed, Cordelia turned to consideration of the matters which seemed to occupy these females. Away from the presence of the gentlemen, they seemed to relax their guards, metaphorically undoing their corset stays and letting down their headdresses, accepting their teacups from Lady Armthea and settling into their corners for yet another endless round of gossip and fashion. Cordelia, who was perfectly accustomed to the role of observer rather than participant in such things, reflected that this scene must be everywhere being duplicated throughout the country at this very moment, and wondered, not for the first time, that a class of persons with so much resource should be so idle, so ignorant, and so dull.

Rather hopefully, she watched Lady Dorothea moving aimlessly about the room, hoping that her future sister-in-law would come and make conversation with her. But it seemed that the young miss, involved in whatever thoughts possess a young lady on the threshold of her first season, rather moodily opened the rosewood pianoforte (in a cloud of dust, Cordelia noted) and sat down to doodle out some melancholy country ballad, lost in a world of her own.

With a great show of her own thoughtfulness, Lady Easton had procured two cups of tea from the hand of Aunt Southbie, and crossed the room in a rustle of silk as she loudly proclaimed her desire to have a private little coze with dear Overslate's future bride.

Cordelia eyed the beauty warily, sensing trouble, but Lord Trevor's advice had not fallen upon deaf ears, and she moved her shawl a little closer to herself, making room on the tiny sofa for the radiant presence of Charlotte.

"You do take lemon and sugar, do you not, Miss Hardy?" Lady Easton asked with a smile that did not quite reach her eyes as she handed Cordelia a teacup brimming over into the saucer. "Oh! I am so sorry— such an elaborate gown; however, I doubt very much if it will show," she said as a few drops fell upon Cordelia's skirt. "Do let me just dab it with my handkerchief." As Cordelia watched, Charlotte rubbed the tea stain into the silk. "There! Well! I have never been so clumsy before! I don't know what has gotten into me—"

"That is quite all right," Cordelia said. "My maid will get it out."

"Oh, I do so hope she will! Such an *expensive* gown— it would be a great shame to ruin it," Lady Easton replied, settling back with that strange little smile. "Of course, I only have these *rags,* myself. I'm just out of mourning for Easton, you know, and it was very naughty of me to come here, but dear Aunt insisted, and after all, it is a family party, and it is not every day that Overslate chooses a bride!" Resting her own cup delicately on her knee, she patted Cordelia's arm, but this time Miss Hardy was prepared for the onslaught, and raised her cup into her other hand.

Thus routed, Lady Easton settled back, looking about the room. "It must be fatigue, you know, although I have run tame at Overslate ever since I can recall, and ought to be perfectly used to these formal dinners. So necessary, after all, when one is not only the head of the family, but also a duke! I daresay, however, that it must all be such a novelty to you, Miss Hardy."

Cordelia felt the barb, but did not flinch. "It is new to me," she admitted stiffly. "But I daresay I shall learn."

"Oh, I am certain that you will," Lady Easton drawled, her eyes as narrow as a cat's. "Americans, from what I understand of them, are quite—adaptable, would you not say?" Her eyes flickered over Cordelia's ensemble, as if mentally calculating the cost of each item. "Particularly, you know, if they have the resources." She delicately sipped at her tea and shook her head. "Of course, I expect you will be wanting to make all sorts of changes at Overslate. I confess I shall miss the old ways very much. Things have always been the same here, ever since I can recall, everything so dear to me! But I daresay you will want to make everything modern when you are duchess. I do hope that you won't redo the state rooms! On public days, people do so like to see history."

"But not, I think, dust and decay," Cordelia replied. "I shall do whatever makes Overslate the most comfortable. It is his home, after all."

"Comfortable?" Lady Easton's little laugh trilled. "Oh, my dear Miss Hardy, in Overslate's station in life, comfort is the last thing one must think of! He has his duties, you know! And his wife, of course, has hers. She must, of course, be an excellent hostess, and a leader of society, and know all of the right persons! But of course, you must, for you will be bringing Thea out next season. Oh, it shall be quite, quite exciting to be back in society again! I do so look forward to the sort of old entertainments we used to have at Overslate House—quite too elegant, Miss Hardy!"

"I fear that I have not had much experience with English society. I do not really care overmuch for balls and parties, you see."

"What?" Lady Easton asked in genuine surprise. "Not care for society? But that is all that there is! Why else would you become affianced to—" She cut herself off, and a crafty look passed over her face, marring her beauty. "But I should have thought that Americans were all the rage in London this season, particularly if they are possessed of your, er, assets, Miss Hardy. Of course, perhaps having Susannah Southbie as a sponsor does not quite allow one to reach the highest sticklers—such a ramshackle household, so full of children and politics, although, of course, no one can fault Beau's ton, at least. Of course, it must have been fortunate for you and Harry that they were able to make you known to each other," she purred.

Good God, how she hates me, Cordelia thought, and the idea struck her with the force of a blow. It took all of her control not to flinch beneath the undisguised contempt on the other woman's face at that moment. How much they all must hate me! But she is spoiled enough to show it. And, Cordelia added to herself, confident enough of her own triumph.

"Ah, I was hoping that you two ladies would find each other's company," Harry said suddenly from behind them, and only then did Cordelia realize that the gentlemen had begun to troop into the room, rosy with port and convivial from their camaraderie.

The transformation that overcame Lady Easton was fascinating to watch. All of the malice that she had been directing toward Cordelia vanished instantly, and she became almost as saintly and feminine as a painting as she turned to Harry and placed a hand over his that rested against the back of the sofa. "Oh, we have been having the most comfortable coze, Miss Hardy and I! I begin to think that we shall arrive at quite an understanding of each other before the end of this visit."

Cordelia supposed that the look Harry gave his cousin was grateful; was it not kind of dear Cousin Charlotte to take such an interest in the poor little American nobody? And, with a sinking heart, she thought that she detected something else there, some look, some feeling that he had never directed toward *her*. "I'm glad of that. God knows, with this pack of loose fish and odd screws, it's important to know that some of us at least, are getting along."

"Oh, just famously," Lady Easton purred.

"Some of us were talking, you know, of getting up a party of the younger people for a ride over the estate tomorrow. I thought Cordelia might like to see my land," Harry said with a smile at both ladies.

"How famous of you! Do you recall how we were both up on our first ponies, and how we used to sneak away from Bolton and simply gallop over the countryside for hours and hours?" Lady Easton asked breathlessly, clasping her hands together and gazing up at Harry. "Oh, how dashing you were then, Harry!"

The duke's lips curved upward, but he shook his head. "I was a nasty, unruly schoolboy, and you swore then you would never have anything to do with me again after I knocked your hat off," he said, laughing at the memory.

Lady Easton joined him with her trill. "Dear me, what a very foolish girl I was then! But we must not bore Miss Hardy with past history, or she might think there was something between us, would she not? Tell me, Miss Hardy, do you hunt? Of course, this is quite humbug country, but I imagine when you are married, you will have a lodge in the Shires?"

"I do not hunt, I fear, and I barely ride at all. I was brought up in the city, you see," Cordelia said in a low voice, watching as the thin, deep line appeared between Overslate's brows, and Lady Easton's smile broadened to show a great many perfect white teeth. "Indeed," she continued, feeling awkward, "I am a little afraid of horses."

"What a great shame," Lady Easton murmured happily. "I adore riding, and I have not been able to do so since poor Easton died! I shall look forward to it tremendously—a good long gallop in the saddle. D'you recall, Harry, telling me what a fine seat I have? Is that wonderful mare still in the stables? Oh, I am quite excited at the prospect!"

"Yes, I daresay," Harry replied with a shrug. "Well, we shall work something out, never fear."

"Oh, I'm sure that Miss Hardy could ride that old mare—even a child could sit Juno," Lady Easton said smoothly. "So, that is settled! How very exciting!"

"Charlotte, Aunt wants you to come and sing," Lady Dorothea said, appearing suddenly with a sheaf of music.

"Will you please, Charlotte? And sing the ballad about the soldier and the raven? I particularly want to learn it so that I may play it at school, and no one sings as well as you do!" There was adoration in the younger girl's eyes, and Cordelia perceived that if it should come to a competition for the affections of Overslate's sister, the beautiful cousin would certainly win hands down.

"What can I say? I am commanded!" Lady Easton laughed with a modest little gesture as she rose from the sofa with one last look at Harry, Lady Thea already tugging at her sleeve. "Will you come and turn the pages for me, Overslate?"

"I think I may be trusted to perform that small service," Lord Trevor said, having appeared from nowhere, with a hooded smile toward Cordelia. "It will be recompense for hearing you sing, my dear," he added with a delicate gesture.

Charlotte made a little moue, but saw that there was no way out. "If you insist, dear Trev, then I shall make you my slave for the evening. But I suppose that is a role to which you are accustomed, is it not?"

Trevor, unstung, merely raised his glass to his eye and regarded Lady Easton through one hideously magnified orb, "Better a slave to passion than fashion, my dear," he murmured, and with Lady Thea chattering gaily away, led her toward the pianoforte.

Harry's eyes followed his cousin across the room, but to Cordelia, his expression was unreadable. She was, however, almost pathetically gratified when he took his cousin's place on the sofa, casually crossing one long leg over the other and lightly, almost thoughtlessly taking one of her hands in his own, completely unaware of the delicious sensation this small contact produced in her heart.

"Now I suppose we are in for it! All the cousins will insist on taking a turn at performing, and some of them are perfectly dreadful, you know. What demon decided that females must include music among their accomplishments, whether or not they have the slightest aptitude for it, I know not!" he said blithely. "But Charlotte has a lovely voice, at least."

And a sharp tongue, Cordelia thought, but said nothing, only wished that Harry would move a little closer to her.

"How are you faring?" he asked when she had said nothing. "Are you ready for an evening of caterwauling and whist? For I warn you that Aunt will be getting up partners for the card tables at any moment! Chicken stakes, at that! These family things can be so dull, but Charlotte can be trusted to liven things up a little."

"I have no doubt of that," Cordelia replied. "She is beautiful, isn't she?" she added a little wistfully.

"Absolutely! Always been a diamond of the first water. I think poor Trevor's jealous, you know. Lord, Aunt must have been in her cups when she placed you beside *him* at dinner; take care with Trevor! He's a downy one, that rogue cousin of mine, and his tongue's sharp as a rapier blade. He and Charlotte have been at loggerheads ever since I can recall, although I couldn't tell you why, precisely. Lord, Cordelia, are you certain you want to be buckled into such a family as this one?"

Although his words were spoken in jest, Cordelia stiffened, turning to look at him with such anguish in her eyes that he was startled into dropping his loose grip on her hand. Of course, he thought, to her way of thinking, it must be very ill-mannered to criticize his relations, for it was upon their goodwill that she must depend if she aspired to climb into the ton. The laughter died from his eyes, and he very proudly focused his attention upon Charlotte's singing.

Standing beside the pianoforte in her champagne gown, illuminated by the soft backlight of a brace of candles on the stand, she lifted her head, clasping her hands before her, and raised her voice in song.

Lady Dorothea's talents for the arts must have lain in other fields than music, for now and again, Cordelia, with a sure ear, heard the girl striking a wrong note, and Lord Trevor was patently bored as he turned the pages of the sheet music and studied his own reflection in the mirror above the instrument, but Lady Easton, singing a simply plaintive ballad that had enjoyed a great popularity during the long years of the wars, a sad, melancholy lament to a soldier gone off to battles in foreign lands, leaving the singer to pine and pray for his safe return, overcame all, and seemed to have captured her audience with her sweet, clear voice and the sentiment of her song. Lady Armthea nodded her approval, and Mr. Hardy removed a large handkerchief from his pocket and was seen to wipe away a tear, but to Cordelia, it seemed that this was a song Lady Easton was singing only for Harry, for from time to time she forgot herself enough to cast long, mournful glances across the room toward him.

A glance from the corner of her eye at Harry's profile did nothing to reassure Cordelia's insecurity; he seemed to be enthralled by the sight and sound of his beautiful cousin.

It was only when Trevor's eyes strayed from the perpetually fascinating subject of himself to bore directly into Cordelia's, through the medium of the glass, and she read his hard, cynical smile that she realized that he, at least, was vastly amused and encouraging her to share his emotions.

With a last clear trill from Lady Easton, and a singularly discordant note from Thea, the little ballad was ended, and the applause which greeted her was more than simply polite.

It was clear that she basked in this sort of adoring attention, for Charlotte, with another gesture of false modesty, needed very little encouragement to assay a more sprightly air, after gently and rather too sweetly admonishing her cousin to attempt to accompany her *en tempo,* for a change.

Lord Trevor smiled savagely at Cordelia, rolling his eyes, and Miss Hardy found it hard to suppress a returning smile.

When Charlotte had run through three airs, Aunt Southbie led the applause for a second longer than necessary, then riveted her icy gaze and frozen smile upon Cordelia. "I understand Miss Hardy plays," she said to the room at large, in a tone which indicated that her expectations of Cordelia's talents were not high. "Would you be so good as to honor us with a song?"

Panic seized Cordelia. Above all things, she disliked being the center of attention, and she shook her head from side to side, all of her tremblants chiming at once.

"Oh yes, play for us, do!" Lady Easton sang out gaily, crossing the room as if to drag Cordelia from the safety of her seat.

"Yes, Cordy! Daughter, give us one of your songs!" Mr. Hardy said, flushed with wine and pride, oblivious as always of his offspring's retiring nature, and anxious that Lady Easton's accomplishments should not outshine his own daughter's.

Harry took up her hand within his own, squeezing

it gently. "Do so, for me! You play so well, Cordelia," he murmured. "You know that you do, and I like to hear you."

Lord Trevor nodded and smiled beneath his eyelids, beckoning her toward the pianoforte, but Harry's request was all that she needed to rise and cross the room, seating herself before the instrument.

"Can't read a note of music, you know," Trevor murmured as he shifted her chair for her, "but if you give me a nod, I'll turn the pages. Buck up, my dear Miss Hardy!" His eyes met her own, and he nodded. "A deep breath, now."

Cordelia closed her eyes, seeing the music in her head. When she was before the pianoforte, the rest of the world disappeared, and she was alone with herself. She felt the strength flowing through her fingertips, the energy gathering about her. Here, at least, there was one place where she knew she did well, and if it would make Harry happy...

Perhaps the Chrisfields had all been watching her with amused contempt, a sort of toleration for her fortune and her status as the future duchess. Certainly none of them, particularly Aunt Southbie and Lady Easton, were expecting such a quiet little drab of a girl to be able to coax such sounds from that ancient instrument. But play Cordelia did, first a little Mozart piece, and then a Beethoven sonata, with more force and passion than even she had expected to find within herself. As her fingers danced across the keyboard, she thought only of the music, of the expression of herself that found so few other outlets, oblivious to the silent respect she was gathering toward her from even her worst critics, unaware, in her self-imposed trance, of the way Harry sat forward, ignoring Lady Easton, who had taken her place on the sofa, of Augustus Hardy's simple, beaming pride, of Lord Trevor's shrewd and triumphant little smile, well pleased with his protégée's efforts and style. When she began a third, unfamiliar piece, Trevor saw that she held her audience well; even Uncle Southbie was listening, tapping his horn against his leg in rhythm to the music. When at last Cordelia had finished with a lingering chord, there was a stillness in the room, and then, led by Mr. Hardy, a thundering applause.

Cordelia was almost dazed; Lord Trevor had to assist her to rise from the instrument and face her audience.

Even Aunt Southbie seemed to allow the faintest trace of approval to enter her glacial expression. "A very interesting melody, that last piece, Miss Hardy," she said graciously. "But I am not familiar with it."

Cordelia felt herself flushing. "I wrote it myself," she whispered.

"Bravo!" Harry called, applauding, and his admiration and approval were all that Cordelia needed to make her happiness.

"Well!" Lady Easton said, rustling her skirts as she stood up, two faint pink spots of color the only highlight of her fine-boned face. "I daresay none of us should dare to compete against Miss Hardy's talents again tonight!"

"Yes," Aunt Southbie agreed, rising from her chair. "There are card tables set up in the Green Salon. You did say that you played whist, Mr. Hardy?"

"Agreeably so," said the merchant prince, straining his waistcoat buttons as he got to his feet.

"Whist? Whist?" Uncle Southbie said querulously. "A game for old tabbies and schoolchildren! Give me a hand or two of deep basset and pound points any day of the week!"

A certain gleam appeared in Mr. Hardy's eyes. "Deep basset for pound points, you say?" he drawled, his innocence deceiving no one. "Haven't played deep basset in many an age, but if you think we could get up a game, now..." He stroked his chin thoughtfully.

"Why didn't you say you played? Come, come, m'good man! We shall break a deck of pasteboard and a bottle of claret!" Uncle Southbie decided at once, summoning two of the older gentlemen to join them. "Must warn you, play with Prinny! Deep stakes, old man, but I daresay you can stand the wind, hey?"

"Aye, but can you?" Mr. Hardy said jovially as they exited into the next room.

"You were marvelous," Harry said as he approached Cordelia. "I could never tire of hearing you play!"

"And I think, I think that I could play forever, if you were there to listen," Cordelia said shyly.

"How perfectly wonderful!" Lady Easton exclaimed, appearing to place a small hand in the crook of Overslate's elbow, as she smiled at Cordelia. "For now that the card players have retired, I have been thinking that we should get up a little dancing!" She made a little pouting expression, gazing up at Overslate. "I have been buried in mourning for a year, and depend upon you to show me all of the latest steps. I am dying to waltz, Harry!"

Around the room, the ill-assorted couples were making up sets. Harry smiled apologetically at Cordelia. "Would you mind? You do play so well, and it would keep them all entertained." Although he spoke as if Cordelia were already the hostess of the castle, humoring the whims of a guest, she could only see it as a rejection of herself in Lady Easton's favor.

"Of course," she agreed with a lightness in her voice that she was far from feeling, and turned toward the instrument once again to avoid having to watch as Harry took Lady Easton in the embrace of the waltz.

Her fingers danced methodically over the keys, however, and it was some moments before she was aware of Lord Trevor reclining languidly over her, his long delicate fingers tracing inlaid patterns in the wood of the pianoforte as he gave her one of his long, cryptic smiles.

"You know," he remarked conversationally, "I have never had any great fondness for my dear cousin the duke. We have, shall we say, so little in common. Such a very depressingly masculine sort of a fellow, all given to soldierings and horses and huntings and boxing and such things. Too, too bloodthirsty!"

Seeing that Cordelia might be bristling in defense of her beloved, Trevor shook his head and touched a finger to his lips. "But, my dear Miss Hardy, I must be honest with you. None of us is to be quite trusted in this family. We are so seldom what we seem to be. Inbred, I suppose. Yes, that must account for it. I came to laugh at this *mésalliance,* and in all honesty, I must say that you disturb me profoundly. Your gown is a tragic mistake in every aspect, you will never be a great beauty, or even a brilliant wit. Not even enough of you to become an original, alas. Your salons will doubtless be known more for their comfort than their style, your balls will be devoted to making certain that your guests are happy and entertained rather than aware of your latest gown or flirtation, your dinners will be known for good food rather than any delicious scrap of scandal, and quite frankly, you will never, barring a miracle, be of any great consequence in the affairs of the ton, despite your fortune and Overslate's title. *But!*" He raised his finger to his lips again, as if to conceal a smile. "While I am perfectly certain that dear Charlotte would enhance the rank of Duchess of Overslate with all of the attributes of beauty, fashion, and power with far more panache than you could ever hope to attain, you, my dear Miss Hardy, just may turn out to be the female who would make our Harry a very happy husband!" He shook his head inside his collars. "After all, stranger things have been known to happen. But, then again, I am not a trustworthy person. The affairs between male and female, alas, have never been mine to comprehend. But despite myself I seem to have overthrown my self-appointed role as neutral observer to marshal my forces to your side of the battle."

Before Cordelia could think of anything to reply to this remarkable statement, the viscount had ambled away to have a look at his Aunt Southbie's hand at cards, an act that so upset that formidable female that she bid three spades and lost her hand, much to her own vexation.

But the waltz had ended, and it was only the matter of a moment before Lady Thea, with a little grin, had ousted her future sister-in-law from the pianoforte, saying that she wished to play *her* waltz, at least, if Aunt would not yet allow her to dance it, and that Cordelia must needs find a partner.

"May I suggest myself?" Overslate asked, and Cordelia realized that he had been hovering nearby, having relinquished Lady Easton to her impatient gaggle of admirers. As he placed his hand upon Cordelia's waist and looked down at her from his greater height, her head barely reaching his shoulder, he gave her one of his little smiles. "You know, you and I have never danced together, Cordelia, and yet we are engaged!"

"I know," Cordelia replied, shaking her head a little, thrilling to the touch of his body against her own, the faint, masculine scent of clean linen and a light cologne not unpleasantly arousing her senses. "It has all been so very sudden—Harry."

"There! At least we are calling each other by our Christian names now. That is better, I think."

They spun about the floor in silence for some moments, and Cordelia was surprised to find that Overslate was an excellent partner, quite as graceful and easy in his lead as even the shyest miss could wish for. Never before had she enjoyed dancing quite as much as that moment in the Gold Salon, with only Lady Thea to provide the music.

"Aunt Southbie has decided that we shall have a ball—more of a country dance, really—in your honor. But I suppose that it will be a dreadful crush, for she's invited half the county, in addition to the family. Have to snatch a moment to ourselves here and there along the course of this week, you and I...."

"Yes," Cordelia agreed, looking up at him adoringly. "Oh, yes! I think that would be very nice, your grace— Overslate—Harry!"

His hand tightened about hers, and he drew her closer to him, a little puzzled, but pleased by the feelings which this little female could arouse in him when he was least expecting them. He was not a man who was used to emotions.

But Cordelia, lost in a haze of bliss, had not lost her fine musician's ear so far that she could not detect that Lady Thea's playing seemed to have undergone a marked improvement between the time that she had accompanied Lady Easton's singing and the lively spelling of this dance.

A little startled, she glanced toward the pianoforte, to see that young miss positively grinning at her in a most unladylike way.

She allowed herself to grin in return before Harry spun her away from view.

Apparently not everyone was on the side of Lady Easton.

CHAPTER NINE

Miss Hardy, deep in a wondrous dream in which the Duke of Overslate played a prominent role, felt a deep resentment at being snatched away from her blissful slumbers by the sound of the heavy brocade curtains of the Queen's Bed sliding open on their rings to expose her to reality.

"Not now, Betty," she murmured, sleepily attempting to hold Harry's image in her mind's eye for just a few moments longer. "Not *now*," she sighed, turning over on her side.

"But it is not Betty," said a voice, and Cordelia, startled, opened her eyes to find Lady Thea Chrisfield perched upon the edge of the comforter, surrounded by an aura of dust motes raised from the ancient cloth's movements. That young lady was smiling at her mischievously, already attired in a blue riding habit, and as Cordelia struggled to prop herself up on her elbows, she glanced hopefully out the window, looking for one of those gray and rainy days for which the English late summer and fall are so justly known, and was disappointed to see a bright ray of sun falling across the floor.

These twin indications that the riding expedition would not be postponed brought her back to reality and caused her spirits to sink a little at the thought of the day's planned excursion, but Lady Thea instantly distracted her by proffering a tray with chocolate and a sweet roll. "No one ever wakes up early here, save Victor and me, because Aunt keeps to her bed until noon, but I decided that I would spare a maid to bring you your tray. Later, of course, there will be breakfast laid out on the sideboard, but this should get you through until you are dressed. Even your nightclothes are pretty," she added wistfully, gazing with admiration at Cordelia's dimity shift, a Parisian affair of embroidered rosebuds and silk ribband trims. "All of my nightdresses are plain old cambric, you know, and Aunt says that is all that is proper for me until I'm out. But then I want to have the most dashing nightdresses, exactly like yours."

With these words, Lady Thea placed the tray on Cordelia's lap, watching with interest as Miss Hardy, striving for wakefulness, poured her chocolate and attempted to collect her wits. Thea, making herself completely at home, leaned comfortably against the bedpost and sighed with satisfaction at her future. "The only person up and about besides Victor and me is your papa, and we all breakfasted together. You are the luckiest female alive to have such a father, you know. Victor and I never had a father—well, of course we did, but he and our mama died so early that we barely recall them. But your papa said that when your brideclothes are made up, I may have a new gown, and he will buy me a pearl necklace as my bridesmaid present. And he says that he will pay for all of my come-out clothes, and I told him that Aunt said that I must wear her court dress, cut down, and he said that I should have a new court dress of my own, even though they cost three hundred pounds! Uncle Hardy—he said that Victor and I might call him Uncle Hardy, you know!—said that when I made my come-out, I would take London

131

by storm, and that I would have thousands of suitors at my feet."

Cordelia, well used to her father's generosity and his liking for lively young people, merely smiled, thinking that Lady Thea was far more like the daughter her father should have had, rather than herself, and pleased to think that at last, the merchant prince had found a lady who would doubtless appreciate his Pygmalion impulses far more than his retiring offspring. Having taken a liking to Thea herself, she was grateful for a providence that had decreed that her future in-laws and her papa should hit it off so well.

"And that is not all. We all thought that Victor, being a younger son, would have to come down from university and take up a career in the Foreign Service, or holy orders, or something equally dreadful, but Uncle Hardy has been telling us the most wonderful tales about America, and he has offered to take Victor into his business. Victor is quite convinced that he wishes above all things to go into the Louisiana Territory and become a fur trader. Uncle Hardy says that it is early times yet for Victor to be deciding what he wants to do, of course, but that whatever Victor decides to do, since we are to become family, he is more than willing to stand the ready to see him have a good start!" Thea smiled radiantly at Cordelia. "You are so lucky to have *such* a papa who is not prosing on about what is due the Chrisfield name, or what is proper or improper, but seems to understand just how it is, truly, and is so very very warm! Oh, it must be a wonderful thing to have pots and pots of money!" she finished naively. "Quite like having a fairy godfather come to set everything to rights!"

Cordelia felt a faint stir of uneasiness, knowing all too well her father's tendency to believe that money could settle any problem. "Perhaps you ought to discuss these things with your brother before you go too far," she suggested. "After all, he may not approve, or he may have other ideas."

"Oh, Harry!" Thea said dismissively. "He never cares about anything but this place, and trying to keep things going. It is one's duty to love and obey one's brother, of course," Thea said piously, "but Harry can be such a dull stick, and whenever one wants something, he always says to ask Aunt Southbie, which of course does no good, because she may be depended upon to say no. Victor says she's a gorgon because she married Uncle Southbie, who is such a loose fish that she feels someone must be a high stickler in the family, but I think she's just a hypocrite, really, because she says it is her duty to stay here and see that Victor and I are brought up properly, but we have been in school forever and ever, and almost never here, save for the holidays, and she says when Harry marries that she will go to Bath, and I hope that she does!"

Cordelia blinked beneath this onslaught, and Thea propped her head up against her hand, regarding her cheerfully. "I do rattle on you know," the younger girl confessed, without an iota of repentance. "But I thought that since you had come to marry my brother, I should like you, for anything would be better than Aunt Southbie, and you are!"

"Thank you," Cordelia managed to stammer, attempting to keep her lips from twitching.

"May I look at your clothes? The housekeeper said that you arrived with trunks and trunks and trunks of clothes," Thea said, sliding off the bed and crossing the room toward the wardrobe, opening the doors without a by-your-leave. "Oh, such pretty things! Much nicer than anything Charlotte has." She removed a morning dress of ivory crepe and Brussels lace, holding it up before herself, turning before the pier glass. Her eyes met Cordelia's in the mirror. "Cousin Trevor says that Aunt Southbie wishes that Harry was to marry Cousin Charlotte," she said casually.

Cordelia sipped at her chocolate, saying nothing, but two pink spots appeared in her cheeks.

"Everyone adores Cousin Charlotte. But Victor and I think she's a sneak. She used to flirt with Beau, then Harry, then Beau again, trying to set them up against one another, you know, just to please herself. Victor says that is not sporting conduct, for Beau and Harry were raised as brothers." She carefully folded away the morning dress, idly paging through the other clothes. "Do you think that I might see your jewels?" she asked.

Cordelia directed her to her dressing case, and it was not long before the girl had emptied its contents upon the bed, exclaiming with a childlike awe over Mr. Hardy's collection of bauble-gifts to his daughter, adorning herself beneath Miss Hardy's amused eye with pearls and diamonds, admiring herself in a hand glass in such a way as betrayed that there was still a great deal of child lurking behind the young lady in Lady Thea Chrisfield.

"How wonderful it must be to have a fortune," Thea sighed, and Cordelia, who really had very little use for most of her treasures, smiled, shaking her head.

"Most of it doesn't really suit me, you know," she confessed. "I'm far too short and squabby to go about decked out like a chandelier. But it makes Papa happy to see me dressed to the nines." Cordelia stretched, yawning a little, but thinking how much she would have enjoyed having a younger sister like Lady Thea.

"I think that I shall marry a very rich man, so that I go about dripping diamonds and emeralds and rubies! It is a great deal too bad that all the family jewels were sold off to pay for the new stables, and very lucky that you have so many of your own, you know. It is so dreadful to be poor. I have an opal bracelet that was Mama's, but Aunt says I may not wear it until I come out." Thea draped a sapphire necklace across the high bodice of her riding dress, and fitted a tiara over her neatly banded hair, studying herself in the mirror with satisfaction. "I look quite exotic. Like one of Lord Byron's dark-eyed houris," she announced.

Cordelia, entering into the spirit of things, agreed, and slid out from beneath the sheets, padding across the floor to her wardrobe. "To complete the effect, you must have a suitable cloak in which to be rescued from a fate worse than death," she said merrily, pulling out one of her own evening wraps. It was certainly the most fashionable garment in her wardrobe, a Parisian creation of apricot satin and gold lamé, richly trimmed in deep lozenges of brocaded peach, caught with medallions of fleur-de-lis embroidered in gold, hemmed with swansdown and overlaid with a brocade and lamé pelerine that rose to tie about the neck in a standing collar, also trimmed in swansdown and lozenges.

Thea's eyes opened wide at the sight of such opulent grandeur. "I only wore it once," Cordelia confessed, "to a banquet at the American embassy given in honor of the king, and I think that I shall never wear it again, for I felt for all the world like a ship under full sail!"

"Oooh," Thea breathed, delighted as Cordelia slipped the wrap about her shoulders, her expert fingers tying up the large lamé bows that closed the wrap, turning up the pelerine to form a standing collar about the younger girl's face.

"There!" Cordelia said. "Now you are the very picture of a heroine right from the Minerva Press! But you should wear a tiara, of course, and a great many bracelets, and perhaps my pearl and coral loops..." As she spoke, she began to drape pieces of her jewelry willy-nilly about Thea, both of them giggling with delight at the picture that the younger girl made, Thea turning this way and that to strike a pose before the glass.

At that moment, there was a knock upon the door, and before Cordelia could open it, Aunt Southbie put her turbaned head through the portal. "I heard stirring, and I knew that you must be awake, Miss Hardy," she began, than stopped, her expression turning into one of horror as she observed Thea, frozen in her pose before the mirror, glowering defensively at her aunt.

"Dorothea, whatever are you doing?" she demanded in glacial tones, closing the door behind her.

"I was only dressing up," Thea replied, pulling the cloak about herself.

Aunt Southbie sniffed. "Really? I find you in Miss Hardy's bedchamber covered with jewels and wearing a garment that is quite unsuited to a young lady. This is not the conduct of a lady, but a hoyden!"

"It was my fault, ma'am," Cordelia said swiftly, receiving an icy look for her pains, a look that encompassed her disheveled hair, her nightdress, and her bare feet with such a marked degree of distaste that Cordelia was suddenly cold.

"I am very glad that I considered it my duty to rise early to be certain that Miss Hardy had passed an agreeable night," Aunt Southbie said, exuding disapproval from every pore. "Else this disgusting spectacle might have been seen by one of the servants! Really, Dorothea, when will you learn that you must comport yourself as a lady at all times? You will be good enough to remove Miss Hardy's ornaments from your person at once—quite, quite unsuitable! And you will apologize to Miss Hardy for disturbing her and using her things, if you please!"

"But I wanted her to," Cordelia said softly. "It was my idea."

Lady Armthea's smile was arctic. "My dear Miss Hardy, such things simply are not done at Overslate! Such deplorable levity and familiarity with a guest, as Dorothea knows, is simply not done! I am certain that you meant well, of course, but we must not put ideas into my niece's head that are unbecoming to the daughter of a duke."

Thea's lip trembled as she stripped off the bracelets. "We were only play-acting, Aunt," she said defiantly.

Aunt Southbie's brows rose. "Play-acting?" she repeated in tones which might have indicated that the two younger females had been planning to embark upon careers in the theater. "Persons who wish to belong to the house of Chrisfield do not indulge in such vulgar antics as play-acting," she pronounced. "We must recall our station in life!"

"I don't care!" Thea exclaimed, her voice trembling. "I don't care what you say—"

"Thea, please," Cordelia pleaded. "Do as your aunt requests, for you know that she is correct."

The basilisk glare was fastened again upon Cordelia, and Aunt Southbie's lips, set in a thin line of disapproval, drew even farther down toward her chin. "I am glad that you recognize that fact," she said in measured tones. "Now, come, Dorothea, and do not annoy Miss Hardy any further this morning."

As Thea divested herself of her costume, Aunt Southbie regarded Cordelia narrowly. "It is necessary to recall at all times what is due the dignity of the Chrisfields, Miss Hardy," she said. "We must make certain allowances for you, of course, being an—American, but Dorothea must learn that her levity is often quite vulgar, and does not need to be encouraged."

Cordelia bit down the reply which rose to her lips, and Aunt Southbie, seemingly satisfied, beckoned Thea to her side. "I understand that you young persons are to ride this morning. I would suggest that you might like to dress, for Overslate is already up and about. And he dislikes being kept waiting."

With those pronouncements, she escorted her niece from the chamber, leaving Cordelia to sink down on the comforter among her spilled jewels, feeling very much like a chastened schoolgirl herself, wondering if there was any way to please these people.

Her spirits were not lifted when, a half hour later, attired in a nutmeg-brown habit of bombazine, trimmed *à la militaire* in gold frogs and epaulettes, a simple beaver cap set upon her head, she joined the riding party in the stableyard, rather dreading the ordeal that lay before her. Cordelia had never been more than a workaday rider, able to handle a docile mare on an easy jaunt over familiar paths, and the thought of being matched against these notable equestrians, the English, was singularly depressing to her.

But as she stepped through the doorway and saw Lady Easton, very dashingly attired in a habit of marine-blue velveteen, cut daringly (and flatteringly), modishly ornamented with lace jabots and cuffs and madeira braidwork, a very jaunty hussar's cap with several plumes set upon her fair curls, seated indolently against the mounting block in the attitude of a queen receiving her courtiers, including the duke, her spirits were even more cast down than before.

Catching sight of her, Lady Easton broke off her flirtations long enough to deliver Cordelia a very superior smile, saying, "Ah, there is Miss Hardy! I fear that I was quite right, and she overslept a trifle!"

Harry, who was in the act of replacing his watch in the pocket of his waistcoat, frowned slightly, and Thea, who had been talking to a groom and stroking the neck of her mount, threw Cordelia a woeful look, while Lord Victor glowered at his brother.

"Not, I fear, as long as I," Lord Trevor drawled as he made his own appearance, barely concealing a yawn behind his hand. His riding clothes were enough to give even the absent Beau pause, and safely diverted attention from Cordelia, for he had chosen breeches of a sunset-yellow hue, white-topped boots, and a jacket of such close cut that Cordelia feared he would not be able to raise his arms to mount the saddle. Again, his shirt points were startlingly high, and for the expedition, he had chosen a purple-and-yellow-spotted kerchief in place of his usual cravat as a gesture toward the day's sport.

Overslate, dressed with his usual military carelessness, raised his brows as his cousin daintily stepped across the courtyard, but contented himself with suggesting that since the party was all assembled, they might as well mount up and be off.

Lady Easton, disdaining the assistance of the groom at the mounting block, through some wiles known only to herself, had Harry to throw her up into the saddle.

"What an excellent seat Charlotte has," Lord Trevor murmured to Cordelia, removing a snuffbox from his pocket and inhaling a generous pinch. The mount Lady Easton had chosen for herself was a skittish, high-strung bay gelding. and Cordelia suspected that she was allowing the beast to have its head as it snorted and pranced about the stableyard solely to show off her excellent horsemanship as she brought the big gelding under control with seeming lack of effort, calling to the others that she was anxious to be off and away on a grand gallop.

"If you please, miss," said a low voice in her ear, and Cordelia turned to confront Bolton, Harry's groom, leading a little white mare. Bolton's grizzled jaw worked. "Miss Thea let on to me that you wasn't much for the horses, so I took the liberty of saddling up Buttercup for you." The old man ran a hand over the mare's white mane, and she nuzzled his pockets inquiringly. "She's gypsy-trained, miss, and looks show enough, but she's as good as gold and as gentle as a lamb."

Cordelia had the strong suspicion that the groom was doing his very best not to lose himself enough to give her a wink, but the knowledge that such a confirmed misogynist as Bolton was on her side was enough to serve Cordelia with a little courage, and her grateful smile was all that was needed.

She allowed the old groom to mount her on the mare, and was pleased to discover that Buttercup was exactly as he had promised—no slug, but a gently trained lady's mount, responsive to her slightest gesture.

Harry, having thrown his leg over his own huge black stallion, reined the big mount over toward Cordelia with a prancing step, nodding at her. "You do not look as bad on a horse as you say," he agreed, and Cordelia had the feeling that he was relieved that she had mastered at least the rudiments of this essential skill. "We'll be seeing some of the Overslate land today, Cordelia, and you'll see the improvements I've been telling you about. It's a hard thing to overcome two generations of neglect, of squeezing every groat from the land without putting anything back, but my bailiff and I have been adapting the techniques of Cook and your Jefferson, and I hope that you will see what could be, what will be, rather than what is." There was a light in his eyes that must always appear when he spoke of Overslate, and Cordelia nodded, interested, as she must always be, in what interested Harry. "And you'll probably be meeting some of my tenants today, also. I'm certain that they're all curious to see the future duchess—"

At that moment, Lady Easton chose to give spur to her mount, racing out of the courtyard ahead of the rest, calling over her shoulder. "Come, Harry! I challenge you to a race! That slug of yours will never take my gelding!"

The duke, with an apologetic shrug, abruptly turned his mount out of the yard after Lady Easton, the sound of their laughter echoing along the pathway through the park. It was only the matter of a few seconds before they were in turn followed by Lord Victor and Lady Thea and the more energetic members of the party.

"That would leave you and me, Miss Hardy," the

viscount drawled, bringing his own mount up beside her, giving her one of his mocking little smiles as he led her through the gate and into the meadow that led toward the park.

Despite his claims to an aversion to all forms of exertive sporting activities, Cordelia could not help note that Lord Trevor was mounted upon a very spirited Arabian, kept under the most forceful rein in effort to keep pace with her own little mare.

The day's weather had taken one of those rare and precious turns, away from the perpetual rains of an English fall. The mists of the morning had burned away beneath the gentle heat of a bright-yellow sun to reveal a green and pleasant landscape, rendered almost tropically lush from the heavy wetnesses, and only the gentlest breezes rustled through the leaves and the grass, with large, white clouds just peering over the horizon of the rolling hills in the distance.

Cordelia, too long confined in the ancient cities of Europe, lifted her head to the fresh air, spurring the little mare into a brisk canter, enjoying this burst of freedom to the fullest.

Following the others, Cordelia and Trevor entered the shady woods of the home park, where the dark, rich scent of the earth and the ferns which grew beneath the ancient trees rose to fill Miss Hardy's nose with a pleasant sensation. Through the low branches, it was possible to catch a flash here and there of Lady Easton's blue habit, and to hear the galloping canter of their horses ahead.

"I see you are a countrywoman at heart," Lord Trevor commented, noting Cordelia's delight in this carefully maintained and very old wood.

"I confess to it," Miss Hardy said lightly. "I have always preferred the country to the town, though I did live in the city."

The viscount made no further comment. Whatever interested observations he might have chosen to make, he kept to himself, merely keeping pace with Cordelia as they rode along the meandering trails in the wake of the others, finally coming upon them in a little glade in the midst of the park where some ancestor had caused an Italianate temple to be erected.

"There you are!" Lady Easton sang out, breathless and becomingly flushed from her gallop. "We began to think that you would never catch up to us!"

"My dear Charlotte, not all of us wish to expend our energy on first gallop," Lord Trevor commented, reining in and removing a lace-edged kerchief from his pocket in order to flick away an invisible spot of lint from his jacket. "Some of us prefer to keep something in reserve."

"La," said Lady Easton in response, tossing her head. "That's for old ladies! Give me a dash any time, even if Overslate did beat me by a length!"

"I could have told you that your gelding was no match for Thunderbolt," the duke said, laughing in his victory. Watching Cordelia delicately picking her way down the path, he seemed to recall her, and trotted across the green to meet his fiancée.

"This is the pavilion," he announced. "My grandfather had it shipped stone by stone from Italy. Of course, it's falling into ruin now, but I am assured that ruins are quite the thing to have these days. Ride along with me and when we come out on the other side of the park, you will see some prime cropland," he added.

Lady Easton sighed. "How well I recall the times we used to spend hiding from our governesses in the pavilion," she said with a sideways look at Harry. "We used to pretend to be Romeo and Juliet, do you recall, Overslate?"

"We were very young then," Harry replied, with a small frown, matching his pace to Cordelia's. "Charlotte, you ride on ahead with Victor and Thea and give Trevor a good gallop. I shall keep pace with Miss Hardy. There are many things I wish to show her, and I am sure that nothing would bore you more than a tour of the farms."

Lady Easton made a little moue, but with a shrug, she went on, leaving Harry and Cordelia to follow the rest of the party.

"I hope that in time, you will come to see why I love Overslate as I do—what a future I can picture for it,"

141

Harry said, as Cordelia watched his profile. "Not just the castle and the home grounds, Cordelia, but the land itself. There's so much that can be done, with a little money and a little time—and then we shall see what modern agricultural methods can do!"

As he went on in this vein, they traversed the remaining length of the home park and came out onto fields where stalks of corn, heavy with ears, waved gently in the breeze between fields of grain.

Oblivious to the rest of the party moving on ahead along the hedgerows, Harry discoursed to Cordelia at length upon such matters as crop rotation, drainage, contour plowing, and other agrarian affairs that were close to his heart and interest. Cordelia, understanding his love of the land, and feeling for the first time in her city-bred life what it must feel like to live so closely connected to one's own earth, was an attentive listener, trying to pick up as much as she could from him. This will be my land too, she thought, and the idea made her happy.

Although Harry was far too polite to mention the small but important fact that it would be Cordelia's fortunes that would restore Overslate to its former glory and bring its vast lands back into a self-supporting state, Cordelia knew this, and was glad to know that the fortunes that had always meant so little to her could be employed in a manner that would bring satisfaction and contentment to her future husband, and she was happy to ride along beside him, listening to his visions of the future.

Her heart was warmed to see Harry so happy—indeed, never had she seen him more as his true self than the first day that they rode along the hedgerows of his land, and such was the nature of her love for him that his happiness was her own.

The running of a West Country estate was as alien to Cordelia's experience as life upon the dark side of the moon, but here she was able to see Harry for what he truly was, a man devoted to his land, a farmer with a simple pride in what he knew that he could wrest from the generations of neglect which he had inherited from his indifferent ancestors. Instinctively, Cordelia felt the same spirit within herself. Overslate, after all, was only a magnified version of her father's own indigo and cotton plantations in the Carolinas, and the running of those had been a feature of her life almost since birth. As the daughter of a financier, she was wise in the ways and means of the Agrarian Exchanges, and she had managed households of dependents since she had come from school. Charlotte might prove to be a better duchess than Cordelia could ever aspire to be. But when all was said and done, she thought, riding beside her man, duke though Harry might be titled, his true occupation was that of a farmer; and Cordelia Hardy knew she would make a very good farmer's wife.

"This is the only thing that is real to me—come harvest time, when you see me in the fields with the reapers, wearing a smock and having you come out in the trap to bring me my lunch, you will see what I mean," Harry said, looking into Cordelia's eyes. "You must understand that, you know. That is the largest part of my life, not the London seasons, nor the foibles of the ton, but Overslate—the land. I know that you care for the ton side of things, and I will do my best for you there, but you must, in turn, understand that Overslate is my life."

Cordelia looked back at Harry quizzically. "But what is yours must be mine also. And as for the tonnish life—"

At that moment, they crossed through a stile, and found the rest of the party rather impatiently attending them beneath the shade of a small copse of birch trees.

"Harry, we are decided that we shall ride on to the barrow," Lady Thea announced. "We thought we would take the route across the tors, and down into the stream."

Harry cast a doubtful look at Cordelia. "Perhaps it would be better to go around by the road. I'm not at all certain that Miss Hardy could handle that rough ground."

"Oh, then I shall ride with her the long way, and the rest of you may have your gallop. I have quite exhausted the first wind from Hermes, and would be per-

143

fectly happy to amble for a bit," Lady Easton said swiftly, patting the neck of her gelding.

"Perhaps I ought to go with you," Harry said, frowning slightly.

"Oh, no! You go on ahead," Lady Easton replied with a little smile at Cordelia. "Miss Hardy and I will be perfectly all right. We shall have a comfortable little chat along the way, and meet you there in a quarter hour."

Cordelia, sensing that perhaps a palm was being held out to her, agreed to this plan, and the two parties soon separated, the majority taking the rougher terrain, Lady Easton and Miss Hardy ambling on beside the hedgerows.

"How very tiresome you must find it when Harry goes on and on about his silly farming," Lady Easton ventured in quite a friendly voice.

"Oh, not at all!" Cordelia replied swiftly. "For it is what pleases him the most, and I am determined to learn everything that I can. I rather like the country, you see." She cast a sidelong glance at the beauty. "Perhaps I would have made a good farmer's wife."

"Perhaps you would," Lady Easton answered agreeably. "They do so much of that sort of thing in America, after all. Personally, I cannot see what pleasure Overslate would possibly derive from being up at dawn and riding about his marshes. It makes me yawn just to think of it. Being stranded in the North Country at Easton Place for the full year of mourning was the most deadly bore. London! There is where the world begins and ends!" she said, giving the plumes in her hussar's cap a little shake.

"Harry seems to prefer to be at Overslate," Cordelia mused. "He is much more relaxed here, much more himself."

"Oh, repairing leases in the country is all that he needs. But he is Duke of Overslate, my dear Miss Hardy, and as such, his place is as a leader of the ton, not buried in some dreary catalogue of plowshares or some perfectly awful cattle auction!" Lady Easton said airily. "And as his wife, it will be your duty to be certain that he does not live like some odious squire, quite

144

covered with mud and drinking his ale out of a firkin."
She shook her head. "One would think, dear Miss
Hardy, with your, er, assets, that you would be quite
anxious to see him relieved of such burdens. After all,
what are bailiffs for?"

"Papa says that a job is done best when done by
oneself," Cordelia replied.

Lady Easton gave a little trill of laughter. "Your
father is, of course, quite an original sort of person, and
one must admire his business sense, but what can he
know of the duties of a duke?"

Before Cordelia could make a reply to this statement,
Lady Easton galloped on ahead for some few yards,
toward the edge of a wooden copse. "Come, this way!"
she called over her shoulder. "It will take us off the
road and bring us out just in time to meet them at the
barrow!"

Before Cordelia could spur the little mare to a trot,
Lady Easton had disappeared into the trees, leaving
only a rustle of leaves to indicate her passing.

Bravely, Cordelia attempted to follow her, but it was
not long before she had lost even the sight of that blue
habit among the leaves, or even the sound of the distant
beating of the gelding's hooves against the soft earth.
With one last mocking trill of laughter somewhere deep
in the forest, Lady Easton was gone.

Looking about herself, Cordelia saw that she was
deeper into the forest than she had first believed. All
about her, the trees enclosed her mare, and there was
no sign of a path or a guidepost to indicate to her in
which direction she should go.

For a moment, Miss Hardy felt a slight panic. Even
on such an estate as Overslate, it would be very simple
for a stranger to become lost, and while it was no vast
and unchartered American wilderness, the thought of
poachers or worse lurking in the shadows made her
shudder slightly. She recalled her father's stories of his
boyhood in Hampshire, when his mother never ventured from home on horseback without the accompani-
ment of a groom, and shuddered slightly. Worse, she
suddenly saw how Lady Easton had deliberately abandoned her, and felt puzzled at such treachery.

But she was a female of common sense, and after some meandering without any trace of a path, decided that the best course of action would be to give the little mare her head, in hopes that she would return to the stables.

In this manner, Cordelia and her white mare picked their way through the glades for some few minutes, until at last, with a little whinny, Buttercup crossed a deep ditch and came into open ground.

Looking about herself, Cordelia saw that she was not, as she had hoped, back at the stables of Overslate, but at the edge of what appeared to be someone's kitchen garden in the midst of a row of neat little stone cottages, each one thatched with a straw roof.

To avoid trampling a row of crops, she reined in Buttercup and traveled along a footpath toward the nearest of these little dwellings, where a small child was feeding several chickens in the front yard.

The child, upon seeing the unlikely sight of a lady mounted on a white mare approaching, froze in the midst of the act of casting out chickenfeed and simply stared, wide-eyed, as Cordelia approached.

"If you please," she asked pleasantly, "where am I? I seem to have lost my way."

The child gave no response to this, but continued to stare at her for several seconds before turning and running back into the house, shouting, *"Ma!"*

"Now what is it?" a woman asked, appearing in the doorway, still holding a rolling pin in one hand and tucking a loose strand of hair up beneath her clean white mobcap. "Jamie, I told you—" Catching sight of Cordelia, she broke off, staring, as the child had done, at the sight of a lady on horseback.

"If you please," Cordelia said, "I'm very lost—I'm trying to find my way to the barrow."

The woman, never taking her eyes from Cordelia, dropped a curtsy. "Barrow's a mile or so that way—" she began, and then from the interior of the cottage, there came a wailing sound, and the woman spun in the doorway, shouting, "The baby!"

In an instant, Cordelia had dismounted and entered the low-roofed dwelling, where she saw, in the dim light

146

of a smoky peat fire, that a toddling infant, taking advantage of his mother's temporary distraction, had managed to upset a kettle of boiling porridge from the hearth, and all over herself.

The woman was stooping over the child, frantically wiping the boiling hot mess from the little girl's face and hands, while the boy who had been feeding the chickens stood by, watching in numb horror. The sound of the smaller child's wails seemed to fill the small room, and the mother, almost hysterical now, added her own cries to those of her injured child, doing, it seemed to Cordelia, more harm, than good.

In an instant, she had stripped off her riding gloves, taken up a rag from the drying rack beside the fire, and dipped it into a bucket of water on the dry sink. "Get me a knife," she commanded the boy in such tones that he ran instantly to obey, and gently pushing the hysterical mother aside, she knelt to sponge away the steaming liquid from the child's exposed skin.

"There now, there," she said in a calm voice, and it seemed to prove effective, for as she worked to remove the porridge from the child's reddening skin, the wails died away into sniffles, with only an occasional whimper when she rubbed the inflamed flesh too roughly.

The boy handed her a rough knife, and she immediately began to cut away the rough linsey smock, covered in red-hot porridge, from the child's skin, working with such rapidity that the little girl did not even have time to cry out as the hot, wet fabric peeled away from her body.

"Tea," Cordelia commanded over her shoulder. "Fill up a tub with water and tea leaves!"

Stunned, the woman obeyed, working frantically at the pump while Cordelia continued to sponge off the inflamed areas of the little girl's skin with the wet rag, talking to her all the while in a calming tone of voice.

When she saw that the tub was filled, she picked up the little girl and gently eased her into the steeping liquid. "Now, if you will just sit there and be still, by and by, it will cease to hurt, and you will be as good as new," Cordelia told her, gently sponging at her

147

tender skin with the rag. "Tea, you see, will take away the burning."

"I can do that now, miss," the woman said, and as Cordelia relinquished her chore to the child's mother, she saw how very young, no more than a girl, really, the other woman appeared to be. "There now, there now, miss has fixed you all up, and a nasty spill that was, too, Lily! How many times have I told you not to go near the fire?"

"I think at that age, they are most likely to do precisely what you tell them not to do," Cordelia observed, and the woman looked up at her."

"I suppose you're right, miss," she said, "but it's hard to keep an eye on one just beginning to walk, and into everything, and still try to do the chores too. Here now, you've gotten porridge and water all over your dress!"

Cordelia looked down at her disheveled self and shrugged. "It makes no difference," she said. "The important thing was to prevent the child from becoming scarred as well as scalded."

"Jeremy, run and get a bucket of water and a clean towel for miss to clean herself off. I don't know what I would have done if you hadn't come when you had—the sight of Lily all covered with boiling porridge was enough to stop my heart, and that's a fact," the woman said, still sponging her daughter with the tea solution.

"It's an ill wind that blows no one some good," Cordelia murmured, more to herself than to her companion, and gingerly, she began to sponge the porridge away from the front of her gown. "I daresay that Lily has had more of a fright than any actual harm."

"I'm that grateful to you, miss," the other woman said. "Imagine, a lady coming along, all dressed up as fine as someone from the castle, and knowing what to do."

"Actually," Cordelia admitted, "I am from the castle, in a matter of speaking. I am Cordelia Hardy, and I am to marry the duke."

The woman's eyes grew as large as saucers, and only her daughter's sniffles recalled her to her duty. "You're to be the new duchess?" she asked, incredulous.

Cordelia inclined her head.

148

"That is something like!" the other woman exclaimed, her manner becoming instantly respectful and curious at once. "You're the American miss that's to marry the duke? We've not seen anyone from the castle down among the tenants since the duchess died. Lady Armthea, she wants something, she always sends the housekeeper. Not one to soil her petticoats among the tenants and never was. But I recall the old duchess when I was a slip of a thing, no bigger than Lily. If there was a birth or a death or a sickness, didn't matter what time of day or night, or even if she were in the midst of some grand affair, she'd come right down here herself, ready to do what she could. Always had a kind word for everyone, she did...." As if she had said too much, the woman stared down at the floor. "Briggs is my name. Amelia Briggs. My husband's cattle chief to the duke. Jamie! Don't just stand there gawking! Hitch up the duchess's horse, and bring down a bottle of my good elderberry wine. The duke's a fine man, miss, if you'll pardon me for saying so, and I wish you happy! Imagine, the duchess coming to our house!"

Cordelia, who detested elderberry wine above all things, busied herself in looking about on the shelves. "What you shall need next is a poultice for the little girl, Lily. Have you any comfrey root? That will boil down quite nicely, and when it is cool, you may apply compresses to her, and it will relieve the swelling and the redness...."

The sun, with the capriciousness of English late summer and fall, was fast fading behind a cloud, and the threat of rain hung in the air when the sound of hoofbeats was heard from outside the little cottage.

"There's her horse!" said a familiar voice. "She must be at the Briggses'!" And very soon afterward, there was a knock on the door.

Mrs. Briggs rose from the table, settling her teacup into its saucer. "There's your duke now, Miss Hardy," she said, "and a long enough time it took them to find you, I must say!"

"Good day, Mrs. Briggs," Overslate said, looming in the doorway, peering into the darkness of the cottage. "I seem to have lost my fiancée—"

"She's right here, your grace," Amelia Briggs said, stepping aside to reveal the sight of Cordelia seated at the table with a poulticed and becalmed Lily resting peacefully in her arms.

"Cordelia!" Overslate exclaimed. "Where have you been? We've been waiting and waiting for you, sure that something had gone amiss—and here you sit!"

"I—" Cordelia began.

"Ah, there she is, the saucy girl!" Lady Easton said gaily as she peered over Overslate's shoulder, shaking an admonitory finger at Cordelia. "It was very naughty of you to run away from me like that! I see that you got yourself lost, also! You should have stayed beside me, as I bid you!"

"We've been searching high and low for you," Overslate said sternly, his relief at finding Cordelia safe and sound with Mrs. Briggs transferring itself, not unnaturally, into the sound of anger.

"Only to find you taking your ease in this quaint little cottage. Well, they do say Americans are democratic," Lady Easton said with a little smile.

"Come, then, it's coming on to rain and we must be back to the castle by teatime! A fine chase you've given me, Cordelia!" Overslate exclaimed impatiently.

Cordelia flushed to the roots of her hair and silently handed Lily back to her mother.

"I won't forget the comfrey poultices, Miss Hardy," promised Mrs. Briggs gratefully. "And I am obliged to you, coming along as you did to save my Lily—"

"Cordelia!" Overslate said impatiently. "Thank you, Mrs. Briggs! Haven't got time to chat—must be back at the castle for tea. My aunt will be in a taking!"

As Cordelia mounted her mare, she was aware of the curious stares given to her by the rest of the party, and wondered how many of them had been taken in by Lady Easton's story. But by that time, she gauged their mood to be of less than the best will toward anyone, in particular herself, and she rode along behind them as best she could, dismally listening as Lady Easton chattered gaily to Overslate.

The rain had just begun to break in a fine, penetrating mist when the bedraggled party arrived in the stableyard, and they very quickly exited into the house, where hot tea and mulled wine awaited them.

Joining in the company of the older persons, Cordelia was made to listen once again to Lady Easton's story of how Miss Hardy had failed to follow her lead along the path through the woods and became lost, only to be discovered again after the most frantic search, quite at her ease in a tenant's cottage, while all the rest of them had been frantic with worry, causing them to miss tea.

Cordelia herself had begun to doubt her own perceptions of the incident, and she hung her head, studying the stains on her habit rather than face the looks of the rest of the company. Not even her father seemed willing to support her cause, for his tea was already delayed, and he was a man who looked forward to his repasts.

"Well, be that as it may," Overslate said, "anyone could have become lost." But in Cordelia's ears, it sounded as if he was trying to excuse her for an act of which he himself was ashamed.

"I think we may wait awhile longer while you all go up and change out of all your dirt," Aunt Southbie said, directing her basilisk glare most pointedly at Cordelia's stained habit.

Cordelia was only too glad to beat a hasty retreat to her bedchamber, and the ministrations of Betty, who instead of offering her comfort clucked her tongue and opined that those grease stains would never come out, not if she were to steep it in lemon juice.

Cordelia's mood was not brightened when she slipped out of her chamber a quarter hour later, rather more neatly dressed in a green dinner dress of olive merino with ruches of bronze lustering at hem and collar, rather slowly moving down the long hallway toward the salons when she saw two figures in the alcove by the window.

"You know, Overslate, that I would never intrude where I thought I was not wanted. But I feel that it is my duty—no, my right!—to speak out," said Lady Easton's voice in low, throbbing accents. As the other figure moved away from the window, in the dim light, Cordelia saw Overslate, watched numbly as one of Lady Easton's arms snaked out about his neck. "But you must think! She is not one of us, Overslate! An American, a mushroom, no manners, no countenance, no style! Can you truly tell me that you can see her as Duchess of Overslate? That ensemble she wore to dinner last night—all those vulgar emeralds, trumpeting off her money! The way she deliberately lost herself this afternoon, trying to disguise the fact that she has no horsemanship, poor dear. And the sight of her, as cozy as you please, hobnobbing with a plowman's wife—"

"Cattleman. Head cattleman," Harry said tonelessly.

"What matter! Come, Harry, I know you! I know that whatever dreadful bargain you've made for Overslate, you cannot, you will not ever be happy with her! D'you know what they're calling her in London? The Dollar Duchess!" Lady Easton's laugh trilled in the passageway, and her other arm entwined itself about Harry's shoulders, drawing him closer to herself. "I know you— I know what you need, what you want—and it is not a wife known as the Dollar Duchess...." She lifted her face toward Overslate's, a mocking laugh flickering across her lips. "We were more than cousins, more than friends once, you and I."

Stifling a gasp, Cordelia turned silently away.

The Dollar Duchess! The mocking phrase rang in her ears, and hot tears stung at her eyes.

CHAPTER TEN

Through swimming eyes, Cordelia looked up at the viscount, her face the picture of misery and defeat.

Lord Trevor shook his head, laid a long finger against his lips and, silently drew Cordelia down the hallway into his dressing room, closing the door behind them.

"Humbert, a handkerchief for the lady, if you please!" the viscount commanded his valet, a beautiful young man of Adonis-like features. "Come now, Miss Hardy! Never could stand the sight of crying females! Makes them look even less interesting, you know! Ah, thank you, Humbert!" The viscount took one of his own lace-edged handkerchiefs from his man and handed it to Cordelia, who used it to dab at her eyes and blow her nose, an action which evidently offended the handsome Humbert so thoroughly that he gave a sniff and immediately recalled himself to duties elsewhere, leaving Cordelia caught between laughter and tears.

"Th-thank you again!" she managed to say.

"It is nothing, really, my dear! Save now I shall have to walk on eggshells with Humbert for a week! A lady in my dressing room! Doubtless my shirts will be ill pressed and my boots will lose a certain luster," the viscount complained, settling Cordelia into the chaise and himself on the stool before the mirror, unable to resist a glance at his own reflection in the mirror. Satisfied that he was the picture of perfection, he shook his head at Miss Hardy.

"Do they really call me the Dollar Duchess?" she demanded plaintively.

Without the least trace of discomfort, the viscount nodded. "Rather original, don't you think? It never hurts to have a sobriquet attached to your name, after all."

"They were lovers," she said slowly.

"On the mark once again! But I hardly think that is anything to upset you! After all, that was before Harry went to Spain—past history! And to my knowledge, Charlotte played Easton fast and loose with half the men in London, smiling like a Botticelli angel all the while at all the high sticklers and old tabbies who worship the ground she treads. Come now, Miss Hardy, you are not an innocent young girl. Do not, I pray you, come missish on me now over a mere trifle."

"I cannot fight her!" Cordelia said in a low voice. "She is everything that I am not! It is true! I have no style, no manners, no knowledge of how to comport myself as a duchess! But I never wanted to be a duchess! If Harry were just a farmer, I would love him all the same!"

"Never wish to be a duchess? Come now, my dear Miss Hardy! Then why—" He broke off, looking at her closely. "You do love him, don't you? By God, you do! Amazin'!"

"Of course I love him! Why else should I wish to marry him? And I thought that he loved me, until—until I saw that scene!" Here she threatened to burst into renewed tears, all the while lamenting her own woeful shortcomings in such a torrent of words that the viscount finally was forced to shake his head.

"Miss Hardy, while I must say that you have garnered more sympathy from me than I thought it possible for me to give anyone, I shall simply have to lose patience with you if you persist in being a watering pot. Here now, bathe your eyes with my lotion of rosewater—quite my own invention, and very effective, I think, in erasing marks of distress from the countenance—and come down to dinner. I am quite, quite famished. It has been an exhausting day, after all, beating about the briers for hours and hours, ruining a decent pair of top boots, listening to Harry prose on and on about how we might find you in a ditch with a broken neck. Very tiresome!"

Obediently Cordelia allowed the viscount to minister to her complexion and use his own silver comb to give a little touch to her hair.

"If you want my advice, Miss Hardy," he said at last, satisfied with his own handiwork, "you will march down there, treat the whole affair as a very good jest, act as if nothing were wrong, and find some way of spilling red wine all over dear Charlotte's head. No, I am jesting about the last, truly. No need to look so horrified. But there is no need to let anyone know what you have witnessed tonight. Among the other virtues a duchess should possess, courage is paramount."

Cordelia nodded, squaring her shoulders.

But getting herself through the seemingly interminable evening was more of an ordeal than she had planned upon. It seemed to her that every shoulder was turned against her, and that even Lady Thea and Lord Victor were somehow distant and cool, while Harry himself, to Cordelia's heightened sensitivities, seemed to be holding himself aloof, treating her with a rigid politeness that only enhanced her sensation of being marked as an outsider by the rest of the family. Aunt Southbie, having sensed Cordelia's disgrace, was almost effusive, as one might be with an unwelcome guest who is soon to make a departure. It appeared to Cordelia that Lady Easton shone more brightly than ever, flushed with triumph, beautiful in a dinner dress of jonquil georgette, attracting the gentlemen toward her flame like so many moths. From time to time, she watched the other woman stealing a glance across the table at Overslate, smiling at him when their eyes chanced to meet, and then her own plain brown orbs would drop to her plate, where a discreet teardrop or two might have mingled with the uneaten portions set before her.

Even when her father could draw himself away from his cardplaying cronies long enough to admonish her to show a little spirit, she was unable to respond, which led, much to her relief, to the merchant prince's idea that she must be suffering from a dangerous fatigue that could turn into a cold. For once she was glad of his protectiveness, for it provided her with an excuse to retire early to the sanctuary of her own bedroom, leaving Lady Easton triumphant in the lists.

Feeling miserably as if she had failed everyone who had supported her cause, Cordelia crawled away to her room to spend an unhappy night plagued by restless nightmares in which Lady Easton figured prominently as a mocking figure, repeatedly snatching Overslate from Cordelia's embrace.

As a consequence, she slept later into the morning than was her usual custom, and was still at her dressing table, in the capable hands of Betty, when there was a knock upon her door, and Mr. Hardy, this morning resplendent in a violet-and-yellow striped waistcoat, entered the room.

"How's my Cordy today?" he asked, his brows beetling as he surveyed his daughter's hollow eyes and listless manner.

With a little effort, Cordelia pulled herself together to receive Mr. Hardy's kiss. "A little fatigued," she admitted, "but it's nothing really, Papa. How are you?"

Mr. Hardy shrugged. "Doing well, doing well, I thank you, daughter. Won thirty pounds at faro last night from that old stick Southbie. Deep player, very deep player, but no match for Augustus Hardy!" He smiled with self-satisfaction. "Shadwell came down this morning while you were still abed with some affairs that needed my immediate attention. Bought out that Barcelona vintage contract, and we shall soon be shipping Damantillado to England and America. Excellent! Excellent!" He rubbed his hands together. "That woman has the whole house at sixes and sevens for this dashed ball she means to give for you—you wouldn't believe that so many persons were needed to hang up a pink tent in a ballroom. Shabby, that's what I call it, and so I told her—flowers, hothouse flowers, and plenty of them, that's the right touch, but—" He shrugged, dismissing Aunt Southbie with a wave of his hand. "Anyway, daughter, Shadwell's brought down the settlement contracts, and I need you to sign them. Just a formality, nothing to rush yourself about," he continued swiftly. "But when you've done with your dressing, come down to the library and we'll have it over and done with."

"Very well, Papa," Cordelia said obediently, her clear brown gaze meeting his in the mirror.

At that point, it seemed as if Mr. Hardy would have taken himself off, but he lingered upon the threshold, watching Cordelia with a thoughtful frown upon his features.

"Cordy, my girl, there's something I ought to tell you—" he began.

"If you please, Mr. Hardy!" Betty said around a mouthful of hairpins. "Just let me get miss dressed, and she'll be down in a minute."

An almost palpable relief flooded Mr. Hardy's face as his unhappy confession was once again postponed. "Very well! Very well! Shadwell will attend you in the library, then, Cordy!" he said, making a hasty retreat.

When, a quarter of an hour later, Cordelia, avoiding a small army of polishing maids and scurrying footmen, intent upon Lady Armthea's preparations for her ball, entered the library, she was actually surprised to find herself glad to see the glum and familiar face of Gunther Shadwell.

"Miss Hardy!" said the secretary, disentangling his long limbs from a chair beside the fire and hastening to her side to take her hand into his own.

"Good morning, Gunther," Cordelia replied with a wan smile. "I trust Papa has not run you off your feet?"

The secretary scrunched up his features behind his spectacles. "No more than usual, but it is kind of you to inquire. You were always thoughtful, Miss Cordelia—but—" He took a long stride back from her, peering into her face with concern. "As one who must always have your welfare at heart, I must speak! Miss Cordelia, you look so pale, so tired—have these foreigners been plaguing you with their intrigues?"

Cordelia shook her head. "It is nothing, really." She shivered slightly, cold. "It is just that this house is so big, and Overslate's family—well, I need say nothing upon that point. I shall make my adjustments, I suppose."

"Poor Miss Cordelia," Shadwell replied, trembling with feeling. "To see you placed thus in such a ramshackle household is not at all that I could wish for! You, who have been brought up to receive, nay demand—every aspect of order in your life, placed thus among such persons—" Shadwell shuddered delicately, monitoring Miss Hardy closely to see if his words had struck home. It would appear that they had indeed, for Cordelia sighed a little behind her smile, shaking her head slightly.

"No, no," she murmured. "It will all come about, in time. It is just that everything is so strange to me—but I shall adjust myself. It is kind of you to think of me, Gunther."

"My thoughts must always be with you," Shadwell replied formally.

Cordelia seated herself upon the sofa. "I believe that Papa mentioned that you had the settlements drawn up and ready for me to sign?"

This was the moment Shadwell had been waiting for. Since the Hardys had departed London, he had employed his time to his own advantages, with the result that he found himself fully in possession of all the facts surrounding the marriage between Cordelia and the duke. For once, Mr. Shadwell's system of espionage had paid him off well, and now he was prepared to make the fullest use of his information.

Carefully, he opened his portfolio and withdrew the documents, spreading them out upon the table before Cordelia.

She glanced over them without truly seeing, and asked, "They seem to be in order. Have you a pen?"

"I think, Miss Cordelia," Shadwell said slowly, "that you might wish to read through these settlements very carefully. As one who has only your best interests at heart, I feel that it is important that you understand the nature of the contract you are about to enter into with the Duke of Overslate."

"Oh, Shadwell, really," Cordelia protested.

But Shadwell laid one cold hand over her own, forcing her to look up at his face. "I think it would be in your best interests, Miss Cordelia," he repeated carefully.

With a small annoyed sound, Cordelia began laboriously to peruse the heavy sheets of parchment, at first casually, and then with a small, tightly intent look slowly coming over her face.

For several minutes, the only sound in the room was the slow ticking of the clock on the mantel, and the rustle of parchment as Cordelia turned the pages of the settlement.

Mr. Shadwell stared into a point above the fireplace, a small self-satisfied smirk playing about his lean features, only to be instantly wiped away and replaced with an expression of deepest concern as Cordelia's fingers rolled the parchment and slid the closure back, slapping it down against the surface of the table.

"Infamous," she murmured. "Infamous!"

She rose from the table and crossed the room, her shoulders stiff, her arms crossed over her bosom. For a moment, she looked out the window at the slope of the east lawns, where younger members of the party were engaged in a game of battledore and shuttlecock, and when she turned to look at Gunther Shadwell, all vestiges of the American nobody were gone from her features. Her eyes sparkled with fire, and her lips were set into a hard, cold line. Never before in her life had Cordelia Hardy looked more to be her father's daughter than in that moment, and even Shadwell, who had expected some reaction, felt a faint prick of uneasiness in the back of his well-set mind.

"Infamous!" Cordelia said a third time, almost shaking with rage. "To think that I love—*loved* Overslate—that I thought that he loved me—" She broke into a brittle little laugh. "And I tried so hard to please him! And all the while, it was not me but my fortunes that he courted! Did he think that he could have it both ways? My fortune to wife and that trollop to mistress? Good God! Was there ever such a fool! And my father—my own father!—selling me like a slave on an auction block to the highest title! Make me a duchess! Dollar Duchess? Dollar Duchess indeed!"

Shadwell could only stare at her. This was a manifestation of Cordelia Hardy he had never seen before, a smallish woman standing to her full height, swollen, it would seem, with a great and terrible anger, icy with self-control and an awesome dignity that the little heiress had never before shown. It was an aspect of Cordelia that she herself might never have known existed had it not been for the events of the past few days, for this final revelation. "Good God! And to think that I cowered before these people, that I allowed myself to be humiliated and despised for my—my Americanness. No manners, no grace, no style! To hell with them, I say!" Her voice was as cold as steel and just as hard, and Shadwell, feeling that his well-laid plans might be shifting away from beneath his feet just as he had supposed that the prize was within his hands at last, squirmed uncomfortably.

"Oh, yes, I can be led, but not driven! Papa never tires of saying that, does he? And he would lead me, like a lamb to the slaughter, into making a perfect fool of myself over a man who cares nothing for me—only my fortune! Well, let him see how well his precious Lady Easton's fortune supports this crumbling pile and his pack of overbred relations, for I will not! The pair of them, buying and selling me as if I were a piece of goods for trade!" She stalked the length of the room. "Make me a Dollar Duchess, will they? We'll see about that! We'll see just how they all feel when that gorgon of a female has her squeeze tonight and Miss Hardy is nowhere in sight! Then there will be a merry scandal, and I hope that I may be ignored by every tonnish female in England for the rest of my life, and bad cess to them all! The Dollar Duchess! We'll see if there's a Dollar Duchess for them to all laugh about after this night's work! Gunther! We are going back to London at once! Only let me pack a few things!"

Mr. Shadwell swallowed. He had expected tears,

160

swoons, heartbreaks for which he could offer the comfort of his understanding shoulder, and the surety of his own hand in marriage to the complaisant heiress. A precipitous elopement, a breath of scandal, and his employer would certainly comply. What he had not expected was a Cordelia Hardy drawn up in wrath, coldly self-possessed and commanding him as if he were a servant to make preparations to carry her back to London by that very evening.

He sensed, however, that to dispute with this Miss Hardy could become detrimental to his well-being, and that now was not the time to press his scheme into action. Thrown into confusion, he could only meekly comply with her wishes.

Indeed, sensing that his own position might, instead of proceeding toward firm entrenchment as a full partner in Augustus Hardy and Company, be in severe jeopardy, he attempted to remonstrate with Cordelia.

"My dear Miss Hardy—I do do think—hardly the right thing to do—" he stammered, for once at a loss for words.

But Cordelia, set in her mind by the heat of her anger, was not to be deterred. "You will be good enough to inform the coachman that we shall be returning to London within an hour. And," she added, pausing in the doorway and leveling a look at Shadwell that might have toppled a lesser individual, "you will not inform my father or the duke that I am departing!"

When, after successfully having managed to dismiss Betty upon some time-consuming errand downstairs and packed a portmanteau with such things as she felt she might need for her journey, Cordelia, attired in a carriage dress of sapphire-blue bombazine, her sable tippets tossed carelessly about her shoulders and a blue and silver shako trimmed with ostrich plumes jammed rather carelessly over her curls, emerged from her chamber to meet Shadwell at the portico, she found that she had yet one more obstacle to encounter in the form of Viscount Trevor, a late riser, only then emerging from his room.

"What? Bolting so soon?" he inquired, lifting his

quizzing glass to his eye and nodding his approval of her attire.

"Indeed I am!" Cordelia said with a spirit that made Trevor take a step or two backward in surprise. "And so would you, if you had discovered what I have discovered today!" In a series of brief, taut sentences, she sketched out the morning's revelations for his edification, and if a smile appeared on the Viscount's face, he strove to conceal it.

"Indeed," Cordelia finished, shifting her portmanteau from one hand to the other, so that she might offer him her own, well gloved in gray kid, "you are the only person to whom I feel the least obligated, my lord! You at least, took my part! You will not tell them that I am gone until it is far too late for them to try to come after me, will you?" she asked. "No, I know that you would not! You like mischief far too much to ruin your sport!"

The viscount took her hand within his own, nodding. "Trust me!" he said. "In fact, if it were not for the joy of watching the fireworks, I should offer to accompany you to London myself. I daresay it will be dreadfully dull here, with Charlotte in possession of the field."

For a second, Cordelia looked doubtful, but she soon squared her shoulders again. "Let her have him! I don't care—no, I do not! I do *not!* If these are the manners of your society, then you may have them! As for me, I want nothing more than the next boat to America!" She bit her lower lip and started down the hall, turning at the head of the stairs to add, "And you may tell him that I said so, too!"

With a rustle of skirts, she was gone, leaving the viscount to linger in his doorway, where he was shortly joined by the handsome Humbert, come to see what the ruckus had been all about.

"Qu'est-ce que arrive?" Humbert inquired.

"Un succès de scandale, j'espère," the viscount murmured. *"J'espère!"*

162

turned her face toward him, her brown eyes wide, as she put her hand against his, cradling it against her face.

"Cordelia, I do love you," Harry said quietly. "I've been such a damned fool. I admit, at first, I wanted to marry you for your fortune, and that was all arranged between your father and me—but later, when I began to know you, I began to love you...."

She shook her head. "I am changed, Harry," she murmured. "You must understand that I am changed."

"I know. But you looked after me when I was sick...."

Cordelia shifted her position a little, so that she was touching him. "That was when I thought I would lose you. After all, you had driven all the way to London after me, in that foul weather...."

"It was because I didn't realize how much I loved you until I thought that I had lost you. Cordelia, I've been a fool—"

"No, it was I who was a fool. But I am not a fool now." Although she spoke in a low voice, it was a voice full of feeling, and she shook her head from side to side, as if she could deny her own feelings. But her hand tightened about his, and it did not take a great deal of effort for Harry to bring her face to his own, for a long, lingering kiss.

Slowly, and then with greater force, Cordelia felt him drawing her toward him, and her own body surrendered to his touch, burning with a new fire she had never known existed within herself, feeling as if she were floating within his embrace.

She sighed, pushed herself away, only to return again, looking into Harry's gray eyes with a little wonder in her own as they found each other at last.

"You know," he whispered into her ear, "you will have to marry me now, Miss Hardy. I have compromised your honor."

Cordelia, nestling against him, suppressed a little laugh. "You only want my fortune." She sighed. "The Dollar Duchess indeed!"

"On the contrary, it is I who have found a fortune

that cannot be counted in money," Harry whispered. "Cordelia, will you be a good farmer's wife to me?"

"Of course," Miss Hardy replied commonsensically. "But really, Harry, you must let me go now!"

"Not now!" Overslate said, pressing Miss Hardy even closer to himself, liking very much indeed the way in which her body seemed to fit the contours of his own.

"But Harry, I must go and close the door! Another scandal would be all that we would need to assure that we are completely beyond the pale!"

"Then let them have it!" Overslate replied. "We shall have one another, and that, my dear, is all that matters."